The Flower Girls

Book One

Prologue

In the United States, about 840,000 children are reported missing each year. This is more than 2,100 children daily, or one child discovered missing every 40 seconds. However, another 500,000 children go missing without ever being followed up on or even reported.

The Flower Girls Trilogy is about three girls of different descent who grew up in Chicago's Southside from the 1960s to the 1980s. The events in this series are actual, but the characters, timelines, and some locations are fictional.

Follow Rose, Iris, and Lily as they find a bond and connection that transcends time. The Flower Girls evolves into something big, frightening, haunting, and timely. The story follows these three girls who become fast friends in the fifth grade. Seeing their lives through the years and in the eyes of friends and family can be disturbing, dark, enlightening, and full of twists. It includes stories of human trafficking, drugs, civil unrest, civil rights, and homicide, and how the girls prevail until they don't.

Detectives Dillon and Valentine, along with police help, factor into the story about the love of family and friends and tragedy. Corruption in the police department is rampant. Before DNA technology and cell phones, finding or following up on these cases was not as easy. A surprise ending leads into the next installment of the trilogy.

Foreword

Human trafficking is a form of slavery. It happens when a person is forced or tricked into working in dangerous and illegal conditions or having sexual contact with others against their will. A person who is trafficked may be drugged, locked up, beaten, starved, or made to work for many hours a day. Girls and women are the most common victims of sex trafficking, a type of human trafficking.

Traffickers control victims by

- Threatening to hurt them or their families
- Threatening to have them deported
- Taking away their passports, birth certificates, or ID cards
- Making them work to pay back money they claim is owed to them
- Giving them drugs to create an addiction or control them, and then making them perform sexually to get more drugs
- Preventing them from having contact with friends, family, or the outside world

Types of work a trafficked person may be forced to do includes prostitution or sex work, farm work, cleaning, child care, sweatshop work, and other types of labor.

Sometimes, a woman may end up trafficked after being forced to marry someone against her will. In a forced marriage, a woman's husband and his family have control over her. Not all people who are trafficked are taken across state lines or national borders.

Human trafficking happens in every U.S. state. In 2016, 7,500 people were trafficked in the United States, and up to 800,000 are trafficked worldwide each year. Half of these victims are under 18, and most are girls and women.

Human trafficking victims can be from urban, suburban, or rural areas and can have varying levels of education. In the United States, most human trafficking victims come from within the country or from Mexico and the Philippines. While human trafficking can happen to anyone, some people in the United States are at greater risk.

These include:

- Runaways and homeless youth
- Children in the welfare or juvenile justice system
- American Indians and Alaska Natives
- Migrant workers
- People who don't speak English well
- People with disabilities
- People in the LGBTQ community

Of those who fall victim to trafficking, only one percent are rescued. According to the FBI, 57.5 percent of all juvenile prostitution arrests are Black children. Through a two-year review of all suspected human trafficking incidents across the country, 40 percent of sex trafficking victims were identified as Black women. In an interview with the Urban Institute, traffickers admittedly believe trafficking Black women would land them less jail time than trafficking White women if caught. Women who experience partner violence pose a higher risk of being sex trafficked. Of women who called the National Hotline, 36.9 percent were trafficked by their partners. (*Source: Rights 4 Girls, Urban Institute*)

Help is available

Speak with someone today

National Human Trafficking Hotline

Languages: English, Spanish

Hours: 24 hours, 7 days a week

TRAFFICKING

Call 888-373-7888

Text INFO to 233733

About the Author

Shannon Price is an accomplished musician, singer, and author known for compelling, dynamic storytelling and performing. With a passion for music that began in childhood, Shannon has always been drawn to the power of music, lyrics, and the power of words to transport readers to new worlds and ignite their imaginations.

True Crime and the plight of children and women are paramount to her endeavors. After being in situations that could have ended up on Dateline or 20/20, her interest in educating people on how to be safe and prepare in the worst-case scenario is of utmost importance.

Shannon's education extends beyond the creative arts. She is a fourth-degree Blackbelt in the martial art of Taekwondo, a well-known boxer, and a personal trainer. Her greatest aspiration in this field is to empower women and help them recognize and harness their strength. Shannon is also a highly successful, globally trained hypnotherapist, further demonstrating her commitment to personal development and the empowerment of others.

Acknowledgment

I extend my heartfelt gratitude to everyone who contributed significantly to the creation of this book. Your support and encouragement have been invaluable throughout this journey.

For True Crime fans everywhere, the events in this book are actual, but the characters, timelines, and some locations are fictional.

Thank you to all who let me bounce ideas off of you and for allowing me the time to complete Book One of this trilogy. It's a labor of love for all those missing children.

A sincere thank you to Amazon KDP for believing in this project and providing the platform for its publication.

Lastly, to the readers who embark on this literary adventure, your interest in my work is the ultimate reward.

Thank you all for being part of this incredible experience.

Table of Contents

Page Blank Intentionally

IRIS 1964

"Hurry up, Iris," her mom called. "This is the first day at your new school. Are you excited to meet new friends and your teacher?"

"Oh, yes, Mom," Iris said. "The fifth grade is going to be so much fun! Do you think the other kids will like me?"

Quickly, Iris appears in her bedroom doorway. She twirls in her new lavender dress with small yellow flowers, white ruffled socks, and black Mary Jane shoes. Her long, curly, strawberry blonde hair makes her look like a fairy—Tinkerbell, as her mom sometimes calls her.

Mrs. O'Brien stands behind Iris, pulling her hair into a long ponytail that cascades into a ringlet with a pale yellow ribbon. Her bright emerald green eyes sparkle as she says, "Mom, how do I look?"

"You look just perfect, Tinkerbell. You're going to make lots of new friends. Now, hurry, and don't forget your lunch bag. Is your brother ready to go?"

Iris called for Max, "Come on, Max, let's go! Mom said to grab your lunch bag."

Max shuffled, his head full of thick, sun-streaked, reddish-brown hair cropped over his ears and parted on one side, with the front hanging down to the middle of his forehead. This made him look like Will Robinson on Lost in Space as he lowered his striking, dark, cobalt blue eyes to the ground.

"Mom, they serve lunch at junior high. I don't want to be that kid with the lunch sack." Max said decisively.

As his mom wondered how he got so tall this summer, she said, "Oh, that's right. It's supposed to be part of the tuition. You kids get in the car. Dad is waiting, and he does not want to be late today. The two of you will ride the school bus home."

"Bye, Mama!" Iris exclaimed joyfully, arms waving while still grasping her school satchel.

It was a cross between a purse and a briefcase, with straps that she could pull over her shoulders and crisscrossing straps in the back, leaving her arms free. She already had everything she needed for fifth grade in that perfect satchel.

"See you after school, Mama!" said Iris.

Max nodded his head and said, "See ya."

Max planned to carry his books and had a smaller leather shoulder bag for notebooks and writing tools. "Mom, I'm going to be able to put all this stuff in a locker for a change."

"Yes, you will! Oh, and Max," said Mrs. O'Brien, "Please keep an eye on your sister to be sure she gets on the right school bus home!"

Max turned to Iris and gave her a sly grin and a nod upward, throwing his chin back to tease her. Iris looked at him and put her hands on her hips as she stuck out her tongue.

For the first time, Iris's family lived in a modest three-bedroom home with a basement and an actual garage instead of a carport. The newly remodeled, moderately sized house had a basement and an attic, which was great for storage. Iris and Max each had their own bedrooms, while their Mom and Dad shared one. The new house had two bathrooms: one for the kids in the upstairs hallway and one for their parents attached to the master bedroom.

The fenced-in backyard was perfect for Max and Dad to toss the baseball, and the front yard was a fine size for playing in and far enough away from the street traffic.

As they got into the car to drive to school, Mr. O'Brien said, "Hey, Max, see what the school basketball team looks like. Maybe you'll want to try out for the team."

"That's a great idea, Dad," said Max.

Iris thought the new house seemed much bigger than the old house in Kansas. "I like it here." Iris thought out loud as she got into the car.

It was 1964, and Iris and Max were beginning a new life in a new school and town. At the beginning of the Summer, they moved to the renovated Chicago suburb of Hyde Park, which Dad claimed had excellent schools, affordable real estate, and a diverse community. The entire family was delighted with their new, intriguing life.

Before the move, they lived in the progressive city of Lawrence, Kansas. Iris's dad had been scouted to fill a good, higher-paying job at a new insurance firm in Chicago. He said it would be a productive move for the family, and saving for the kids' college would be much easier.

"Are you as excited as I am to see the Cubs play this spring? Mr. O'Brien asked.

Max said, "I can't wait, Dad! Can we put up the basketball hoop

I'm getting for my birthday in the driveway this weekend?"

Mr. O'Brien nodded and said, "Sure! Then, you can invite any new friends who want to come over and shoot some hoops."

Iris said, "Me too! I want to play!"

Max turned to her and said, You're too short."

Iris giggled and told him, "Watch out, Max, I bet I can jump higher! And I want to see the Cubs too, Daddy!"

Iris, who was starting the fifth grade, and her big brother, Max, who was in the seventh grade this year, didn't know what to expect from their new school.

Max, age twelve (almost thirteen, as he corrected anyone who said twelve), seemed more apprehensive than Iris. Kids his age could be hard to make friends with at a new school. Iris, who had turned ten in June, was ready to meet everybody.

During the summer months, while settling into the new city, Iris and Max made some friends around their neighborhood. Some of them would be attending the same school. Some were older, and some younger. Making new friends her age meant a lot to Iris after leaving her close fourth-grade friends in Kansas. Those were the friends she had known all her life. But Iris felt like a new world was about to open up.

With her face beaming, Iris skipped up to the entrance doors, ponytail swinging. Max deliberately walked a few steps behind Iris, feeling a little uncertain. Max had never been a shy kid until now. Now, everything was so different.

Iris turned to look at her brother. "Come on, Max, come on!" she said as she bounded into the school's front hallway, signaling Max to come closer.

Three teachers were at the entrance to each section of the hallways to help guide the students to their correct classrooms as they entered. Max went in one direction to the junior high section, and Iris went to another section for kids in grades one through six.

Iris looked around the fifth-grade classroom with wide eyes. "OOO, it is so bright and cheerful," she said quietly.

On the bulletin boards and walls were colorful letters and posters about books and music. The teacher, Mrs. Adams, was a pretty, dark-haired woman of about thirty-eight with a warm smile and white-rimmed glasses. Iris thought the few gray streaks in her hair looked like moonbeams. Mrs. Adams loved seeing her students' progress each year as they followed their scholastic and artistic endeavors. In parent-teacher meetings, she said this made her students happier, well-rounded adults later.

There were three big shelves of books, including Junior Scholastics Books to Grow On and Books to Discover. A few instruments hung on one wall, including a violin, trombone, and acoustic guitar. A large harmonica was on the top of the bookshelves to the left, and a smaller one was next to it.

Against the wall, next to the chalkboard, there was a time-worn, well-used upright piano. Mrs. Adams would play that old piano or the guitar as the kids learned and sang Americana folk songs like 'This Land Is Your Land', 'Blowing in the Wind', 'If I Had a Hammer', and 'Where Have All the Flowers Gone'. It was no wonder that the kids in Mrs. Adams's classroom were always excited and happy to start each day.

The first thing on the daily class schedule was to say the Pledge of Allegiance, and then the class would sing 'This Land is Your Land' while Mrs. Adams played the guitar. This joyful class of happy fifth-graders was perfect, thought Iris. And she fit in happily and perfectly.

Iris was awestruck as she looked around the room and at the other twenty-four kids in her class. In her school in Kansas, only fourteen kids, including herself, were in her class. One of the girls in the row next to her smiled and waved at Iris. Well, this made her day. As she waved back, Iris listened closely as Mrs. Adams did roll call to hear everyone's name, especially the girl in the next row.

"First Row: Robert, Sammy, Joy, Beth, Betty, Row two: Peggy, Henry, Kathy, Iris, John. Row three: Rachel, Amy, Steven, Lily, James." Iris stopped listening, and Mrs. Adams's voice drifted off. She heard the name Lily. Iris thought: "Lily, her name is LILY! A flower name like mine!"

As Mrs. Adams finished the rest of the roll call, she told the class to open their first textbook of the year: Social Studies! Iris whispered, "I love social studies and history!"

They also started on their new science and math books as the morning went on. By then, it was lunchtime. Iris was looking all around the cafeteria for Lily. Before she could turn around, someone tapped Iris on the shoulder.

"Hi, my name is Lily. I'm in Mrs. Adams' class with you. Would you like to sit with me and another friend at lunch?"

Iris couldn't contain her joy over this. "Yes, I really would like that," Iris said.

Lily was a small, beautiful girl with dark, almost black, deep-set, almond-shaped eyes that reminded Iris of the cups of coffee her mom and dad had every morning. Lily had long, shiny black hair in two braids resembling thick silk rope. She always wore one braid over her right shoulder and one down her back or both braids in front of her shoulders. Her summer sun-kissed complexion made her look like a tropical princess to Iris.

"I love your dress," said Iris. Lily was wearing a pretty aqua and white dress with a matching headband.

"Oh, thank you," said Lily. "I love yours too."

As the two new friends moved to a table where some other kids sat, Lily told Iris, "My family moved to Chicago in 1961 from Osaka, Japan. I started school here in the middle of the first semester of second grade. I liked this school from the day I walked in!"

Lily's father had been transferred to the United States for his work in chemical engineering, but Lily didn't know what that meant or what he did exactly, and he never spoke about it. Lily's mother stayed home and cared for everything in their small, happy family.

Lily told Iris, "The principal had a meeting with my parents when we first came here. He thought I should skip a grade or two since I was scholastically ready for a higher grade level. But my parents did not approve of me skipping to the third or fourth grade. They said I needed to make friends my own age. I'm glad it turned out that way."

"Me too," said Iris, "because I got to meet you, and we can be in class together." The two new friends giggled.

They sat down with a few other kids, and Lily introduced Iris to her friend, Rose.

Lily told Iris, "This is Rose, my best friend! We met in the second grade when I came to this school."

"Hello, Rose," said Iris, smiling and waving across the table. "You have a flower name, too!" Her fingers were interlaced under her chin.

Rose smiled and reached across the table to shake Iris's hand. "We are The Flower Girls!" said Rose, and all three girls clapped and giggled, but not loud enough for the lunch room monitors to hear them. They were sure that a new special bond had just formed between them.

"Rose has a different teacher, and her classroom is in the trailer behind this building, but she is in our same grade," explained Lily.

"I'm so happy to meet you both today," said Iris.

Rose had the smoothest milk chocolate skin Iris had ever seen. Her licorice black hair was artistically twisted and secured with small, bright, colorful barrettes and clips. Rose's eyes were beautiful, big, and bright, like the golden, amber-colored stones in the earrings Iris had seen at the jewelry shop her mom took her to a few weeks ago.

"I can't wait to tell my mom that I met you both today," Iris gleefully proclaimed.

The cafeteria bustled with kids chattering, lunch pails clanging, and paper lunch bags crinkling. "Anyone want to share or swap?" asked Lily.

"I have an oatmeal cookie to swap," said Iris quickly.

Rose raised her hand and said, "I love any kind of cookie! Would you like to swap for my apple?"

"Sure", said Iris. Then she noticed Rose only had an apple and half a peanut butter sandwich for her lunch. She thought for a moment, then asked, "Rose, do you want some of the carrot and celery sticks my mom had packed in my lunch? She always packs way too many for me!"

Rose smiled joyfully and said, "Thanks, Iris! I would love that. Carrots are my favorite!"

Iris thought she had just lassoed the moon with these new friends. As the bell rang to signal the end of lunchtime, the three new friends were overjoyed and couldn't wait until classes were over so they could be together.

"See you after school," said Iris to Lily and Rose. They smiled and waved to each other.

At the end of the school day, they all met outside at the bus line. Rose got onto a bus different from Iris, Max, and Lily.

"Bye, Rose! I'll see you tomorrow!" Said Iris, waving.

"Bye, Rose, see you tomorrow too!" Lily said as she skipped onto her bus.

THE FLOWER GIRLS 1966

As the school year continued, the three friends became inseparable, and everyone called them The Flower Girls. They were always together, no matter what anyone thought or said. When people saw how inseparable they were, the three friends knew they were meant to be together forever. Their parents were overjoyed that this extraordinary friendship had transpired.

Sometimes, when the girls met for a walk around town or to the park, they were told to stay together and not separate in different directions. The parents always planned that one of them would pick the girls up at the painted red wooden picnic table and matching bench in the middle of the park on the open concrete path.

On one such occasion, the flower girls walked through the swings and monkey bar area to play before going to the park bench where Iris's mom would pick them up at the designated time. This day, as the girls sat on the bench waiting for Mrs. O'Brien, an older woman sat beside Iris.

Her white hair was knotted tightly into a bun on the top of her head and secured with a knitting needle. The woman had a bag of knitting in her lap. She glanced at Iris, Lily, and then at Rose. The woman said something under her breath, but Iris didn't quite understand or hear her.

"What did she say?" Iris whispered to Rose.

"I couldn't hear her," said Rose.

"I don't know what she said," Lily told her friends as she shook her head and shrugged her shoulders.

Then, the woman gave Rose a tentative look. Iris and Rose tilted their heads together and giggled. Lily put one hand to her mouth so she could hide her laugh.

Lily followed apprehensively. "Do you think she noticed my birthmark and it made her uncomfortable?"

"No, I don't think so," Rose whispered to Lily.

The woman then pointed one of her knitting needles at the three of them and shook it up and down, and side to side, as if to warn them. The girls all looked away and then decided to cross the street. The woman scowled as she watched them.

Mrs. O'Brien pulled up just in time. They hurried into the backseat of the metallic plum-colored 1960 Chrysler Imperial and told Iris's mom what had happened.

"Mom, do you see that lady on the bench knitting?" Iris asked.

"Yes," said Mrs. O'Brien. "Why? Did something happen?"

"Well, Mom," said Iris. "She was kind of rude and strange to us. She said things under her breath and shook her knitting needles at us. It made us feel weird, but we didn't say anything."

Rose said, "She never smiled, and we felt funny. That's why we crossed the street, Mrs. O'Brien."

"I see," said Mrs. O'Brien.

"I was worried that my birthmark made her nervous or mad or...something," said Lily.

Mrs. O'Brien smiled into the rearview mirror and told the girls,

"Sometimes, people can be confused at how children can be so different but so much alike at the same time. Just like the three of you. You are like three peas in a pod, and I love you."

Iris wondered what her mom meant when she said they were different but the same. The girls shrugged it off, but they still thought about it.

"I only see my best friends. We are all the same, of course," said Iris.

In the eyes of these children, they saw nothing but how much they were the same and loved being together.

LILY 1966

Lily Sato was born in Osaka, Japan, on February 14th, 1954. She was an only child in a loving but strict family. In the spring of 1961, her family moved to the United States, where her father began a new job at Dow Chemicals. He was not allowed to speak to his family about his work as a chemist, so Lily didn't know what he did there, and as an artistic and musical child, it didn't concern her.

She was more interested in drawing, singing, violin, piano lessons, and television shows like Captain Kangaroo, her favorite. She also loved The Flintstones, Bugs Bunny, and Dudley Do-Right. Her parents made sure she watched Mr. Wizard to hone her interest in science and mathematics.

Lily wasn't quite as interested in that as she was in storytelling and making up real lives for her well-loved cartoon characters from age four. She began writing stories about them at age five and drawing pictures of them as if they lived in her neighborhood.

She pretended to interview them like the news reporters she had seen on television. She asked them about their lives and events and pretended to change her voice as each character answered them.

She pretended to interview George Jetson and Fred Flintstone together. She wondered if George Jetson's life was something that Fred Flintstone and his family looked forward to in the future. Then, she would take notes, reviewing what she imagined they told her.

Lily was born with a port-wine stain birthmark that started behind her right ear in the shape of a heart and spread down her neck to her right shoulder. In some areas, it was dark pink, and in others, it was deep red. Lily always wore her waist-length black hair over her right shoulder to hide it. Her mother told her it made her unique and beautiful, and since she was born on Valentine's Day, it was in the shape of a heart, which means she is filled with love.

But Lily certainly did not agree. Some of the kids in school teased her about it incessantly.

Lily's home was spacious, spotless, and smelled like her mother's delicious food. Lily was an only child and had a bedroom all to herself. She used the small hallway bathroom that her mother always made to look bright and sunny.

They had a laundry room downstairs, just off the basement family room, where Lily watched her favorite television shows. She took notes about everything she saw.

She did all her school work in her bedroom at a petite, white-washed desk with a chair just her size. Her violin, music stand, and sheet music from the school orchestra were in her room. She practiced piano lessons on the family's Baldwin spinet piano in the family room.

An Encyclopedia Britannica set and Webster's Dictionary were on the shelves, and posters of her favorite singers and dancers were on the lavender/gray bedroom walls. This color felt cool and warm at the same time.

She also mounted newspaper clippings of Lisa Howard and Barbara Walters, her favorite news reporters, on the white framed bulletin board over her desk.

Meeting Iris at school and introducing her to Rose was exciting for Lily. She had a small handful of friends at school. Some kids avoided her because of her birthmark, but that never stopped Lily from pursuing her hopes, dreams, and creativity. It gave her more time to focus on her future, not what her parents wanted her to do, which was to become a doctor or research scientist.

As sixth grade approached, and then junior high school, her parents spoke to her about her time management.

"Lily, we're so happy you have such good close friends. Now that you are getting a little older, your father and I are putting some time restrictions on your friend visits together due to your instrument practice schedule, reading, and schoolwork time," Mrs. Sato told Lily.

"The time limit for the flower girl get-togethers will be thirty to forty-five minutes unless you are all doing schoolwork together."

They have always loved doing school work together. The three girls helped each other as they talked and laughed the time away.

Lily loved her parents but, at times, felt lonely. She was so happy that her parents let Iris and Rose come over to do homework, play records, dance, and talk and giggle about everything, even if it was only forty-five minutes. To her, it was magic. Her father drove to the Southside to pick up Rose for a Flower Girl date at the Sato's house on some Saturdays. And Iris was close enough to walk or bike over.

Lily's birthmark never mattered to Rose and Iris, and Lily didn't mind them seeing it or asking about it. It was just part of who she was.

"I was born with it," Lily would say.

Iris asked, "Does it hurt?"

Lily replied, "Oh no, it doesn't ever hurt."

Rose would say, "I think it makes you prettier, like a painting. Especially since it is in the shape of a heart behind your ear."

Music, fashion, sports, and relationships became apparent to these friends as they reached the seventh grade. Lily and Rose ran on the middle school girls' track team. Rose was the fastest runner on the girls' team.

Iris, the tallest of the three, preferred girls' basketball. They went to each other's events and cheered for their best friends.

Everyone knew about The Flower Girls and their friendship. Their joy and happiness in life and being together attracted others as they joined them for school events, study groups, and hanging out. However, it also caused jealousy among some other junior high school girls.

"Do you know those two blonde girls standing over there who are a grade ahead of us? They're always staring at us," Lily told Iris and Rose in the lunchroom.

"Their names are Jessica and Julie," said Rose," but I don't know them very well. I've heard how they talk to other girls, and it's not very nice."

Lily replied, "They've started to follow me in the hallways between classes, saying things like, 'You sure don't look like a flower,' 'What is that thing crawling up your neck?' 'Did you burn yourself? Maybe you should wash that off.' It makes me feel self-conscious."

Iris said, "I heard those girls are the mean girls in school. Everyone knows them and steers clear of them as much as possible. That's why they are always together and picking on people."

"They have one small clique of girls that follows them around like a gang of rats," said Rose. "I am surprised they have any friends at all."

One chilly afternoon in the schoolyard, Lily sat on a swing in the sun, head down, holding onto the chain of the swing with one hand and a book she was reading with the other. Her long braids hung over her shoulders, and she felt the sun warm her body.

Julie and Jessica approached her, grabbed the chains of the swing, and began to push Lily back and forth with too much force.

Lily said, "Stop, I'm trying to read. What are you doing here?"

As Julie laughed, Jessica said, "Keep reading. Nobody is stopping you, Kool-Aid face."

"Stop it," yelled Lily.

Rose overheard Lily and ran to the swings. "Hey, Jessica, leave her alone," she shouted.

As Jessica and Julie turned to look, Rose grabbed the swing's chains and said, "Lily, jump off."

Watching this interaction, the playground monitor hurried over to see what was happening.

"Hey, what's going on here, Julie and Jessica?"

Jessica said, "Nothing, Miss Green, she was sitting on my swing. I always use this swing, and they know it!"

Rose replied, "These swings are for anybody to use."

Miss Green, the playground monitor, who was also the eighth-grade English teacher, had been watching and listening. "Go inside to the office, Jessica and Julie, and I will meet you there in five minutes," said Miss Green. "Now!"

Miss Green told Lily, "I'm sorry they were bothering you. It can be dangerous, and they don't even realize it. They are old enough to know better. I will be sure they won't bother you or your friends anymore, and I will call their parents. This isn't the first time their parents have been notified about a problem with those two."

Lily replied, "Thank you, Miss Green. I appreciate it! I don't know why they are like that, but I hope they stop picking on other girls!"

Miss Green nodded, and as she turned to go to the school office, she said quietly, "I hope those two grow up to become kinder to people."

Near the end of the school year 1966, Lily never saw Jessica again, and Julie stopped attending school. Word on the gossip trail was that Julie ran away, and no one had heard from her since the end of April. Or maybe they both got in trouble and were arrested or something.

Word on the street was widespread about what happened to Julie. Everyone was sure she was a runaway, but it was never investigated or proven. Her parents were still searching for her, searching for clues with little assistance from the police.

Jessica's family moved to Wisconsin, where she started a new school. Whatever happened, they never bothered Lily again, and no one had ever heard from Julie or Jessica after that school year.

ROSE 1964-68

Rose, her mom, and her three sisters settled into a small, run-down apartment on the Southside. Mrs. Williams and her daughters kept it as clean and livable as possible, considering there was a bedroom and another smaller room, one bathroom, a miniature living room, and a kitchenette, as the landlord called it. It was painted all light gray with no other color anywhere. The appliances were white but very used, with some dents, streaks, rust, and stains that would be there for eternity.

The landlord never fixed anything, not even a leaky pipe or a toilet that stopped flushing. But when Mr. Williams was alive, he was very handy and seemed able to fix anything.

Mice sometimes raced and skittered across the floors, and occasionally, they would find a rat or two in the cupboards. The family was cautious and kept all the food in containers, but that didn't deter the rodents for the most part. The family had to always wear shoes just in case a mouse or rat decided to nibble on their feet in the middle of the night, or if someone got up to use the bathroom.

The family was limited to living in specific black neighborhoods. They also faced discrimination when attempting to purchase a home after the youngest was born, so they decided to do their best with this tiny kitchenette apartment.

In the early 1960s, black women with high school diplomas were allowed to leave domestic service work, such as housekeeping and cooking, for higher-paying jobs as secretaries, typists, and stenographers. College-educated women could move into managerial careers in the public sector. Mrs. Williams had a high school diploma and secured a solid clerical typing position for a military contractor working with Dow Chemicals.

The Williams family grew quickly with four active daughters: Denice, Maymie, Rose, and June. Mrs. Williams worked three days a week for six to eight hours and was expected to fill in for anyone who called in absent on any given day.

Mr. Williams worked for the railroad and was gone from sunup to sundown on most days of the week. He was strong, tall, and handsome, and loved his family.

The daughters were expected to be home directly after school, and if they were working, they were expected to be home immediately after. Someone was always home to care for the youngest, June, and it was usually Rose. She was two and a half years older than June and loved caring for her. They would play games, take walks, play in the nearby park, and giggle like best friends.

Mrs. Williams clearly stated, "Our house rules are that everyone is to be home before your daddy gets home from work. No excuses!"

The older sisters were also expected to help cook, clean, and keep up with their schoolwork and part-time jobs at the local diner. Rose was the third-born child.

Rose's two older sisters, Denice and Maymie, who were four and three years older, helped the family by getting jobs as cooks and dishwashers at the local diner, Tony's Family Diner, when they turned thirteen and fourteen.

Per Tony and Mrs. Williams' agreement, they were allowed to work only two hours after school and four hours on Saturdays. And that was just enough to help with groceries and necessities and still complete their homework and chores.

The older sisters had to walk to school or take the segregated school bus system. They would then walk from school to work and from work to home. They made it a rule never to walk home or take a bus alone. They would wait for each other or walk with friends.

Rose and June took the school bus and came home right after school. After they were home, Rose was instructed to lock the door and not leave the apartment for any reason. If someone knocked, they were not to answer the door.

However, Rose took June for a walk through the park on nice days. They made it a rule for themselves to stay only long enough to swing for a few minutes and walk around the park once, then head straight home.

On the days Mrs. Williams was not at the office, she helped neighbors with laundry, babysitting, and cooking. By staying close to home on those days, she could always pay lots of attention to the two younger sisters. It was a good routine for the family and was rarely disrupted.

The sisters loved their father, Eddie Williams, who worked all week on the railroads. He was their hero. On Friday and Saturday nights, Eddie performed at a Southside jazz club, playing the piano for his group and other jazz and blues groups traveling into Chicago from different cities and states.

The club was one of the first to allow integrated patrons. Eddie's heart and soul lived in his music, and he earned a little extra income with good tips so the family could have one or two gifts for birthdays or holidays. This was his way of shaking off the grinding railroad work from the week.

When Eddie Williams disappeared, Mrs. Williams was overcome with grief and anger. June was only four when Eddie never returned from his jazz club gig one Saturday night in 1961.

The club where Eddie performed was one of the few that welcomed mixed couples. That night, a white woman, about twenty-two, who frequented the place with her upswept smooth honey blonde hair and frosted platinum streaks, perfect makeup, and big brown doe eyes with long thick lashes, wearing a glittery black dress, rhinestone, and diamond bracelets and earrings, and a choker necklace with a gold heart surrounded by rubies, was with Raymond Davis, a close friend of Eddie's.

On a set break, Eddie went over to say hello to them.

"Hello there, Ray. Hope you're enjoying the music," said Eddie. "And who, may I ask, is your friend?" He had seen the two of them there before, usually alone at a table near the back.

Raymond replied, "Delores, meet my good friend, Eddie Williams. Eddie is not only a talented music man but also works full-time for the railroad and has a family of beautiful women."

Delores smiled and asked in a slight Southern drawl, "A family of beautiful women?"

Eddie said, "Yes, I have a lovely wife, Pearl, and four magnificent daughters."

Raymond said, "You're a lucky man, Eddie Williams."

Delores nodded and said, "Why yes, you are, Mr. Williams." Delores winked at Raymond.

Eddie smiled, tipped his favorite hat, and said, "Nice to meet you, ma'am."

Delores replied, "Oh, Mr. Williams, the pleasure is all mine."

As he left the table to play another set, Raymond pulled Eddie aside to tell him something private. Eddie listened and nodded.

Then Delores extended her hand toward Eddie, her wrist and fingers pointing down. He gently took the tips of her fingers and nodded, again, tipping the brim of his hat to acknowledge her gesture.

"What a beautiful pinky ring," said Delores, noticing the ring on Eddie's left pinky finger.

Eddie said, "Why, thank you, Ms. Delores. It was my father's. His name was Edward Williams, the second."

Delores smiled and said, "Well then, you must be Edward Williams, the third."

Eddie smiled and nodded, then walked back to the stage for the last set of the night. A peculiar feeling engulfed him as he walked away from the table. As soon as he thought about his gesture of taking the woman's hand, his heart sank. Eddie whispered so no one could hear, "Now, why did I do that?"

He had always known not to touch a white woman, especially if she was with another black man. But she was friendly and reached her hand out to Eddie first, and, being a gentleman, he automatically acknowledged that. And after all, Ray was his best friend.

At the end of the night, after the last set, Eddie took off his favorite dress hat and hung it on a hook by the back door. He pulled on his jacket and went out to have a smoke while the other musicians were packing up their instruments. It was shivering, wet, cold, and starting to sleet. Eddie didn't have his rain hat or a hood on his jacket, so he quickly headed back inside.

Suddenly, as Eddie turned to go inside, he was yanked back hard. "Not so fast," he heard a deep voice say.

Eddie was brutally attacked by a group of three men, two white and one black, whom he thought saw him speaking to the white woman and Raymond in the club.

Eddie was a tall man, strong and muscular from his work on the railroad. But he didn't see this coming. They attacked him from behind, and as he tried to fight back, he lost his footing and was overpowered. All three men wore hats and oversized jackets so that he couldn't recognize them.

"Stop, who are you? Why me? What do you want?" cried Eddie.

The men had clubs and bats, and one had a switchblade. Eddie was beaten, bludgeoned, stabbed, kicked, and left in a pool of blood, barely breathing, when the three attackers fled.

Inside, the nightclub owner, Tony Rossini, asked Raymond and the wait staff, "Have you seen Eddie? I want to pay him and give him his tips for the night."

Raymond said, "Looks like he went out back for a smoke, but he left his hat hanging on the rack. Want me to check?"

Tony replied, "No thanks, I'll go out and see." Tony grabbed his rain jacket from the hook inside the door, put up the hood, and walked out the back door.

He was taken aback by the horrific sight. Tony, a retired sheriff, had seen a lot over the years, but Eddie is one of his best friends and business partners.

Tony ran back into the club. "Call the cops. Something happened to Eddie. Call now!"

The bartender immediately called the police station without hesitation, but it took a long time for any police to arrive.

Raymond and Delores slipped out the front door, trying not to cause a commotion because they were a mixed-race couple.

Law enforcement didn't prioritize crime in Southside black neighborhoods, especially after dark. One squad car finally approached the scene and saw Tony hunched over Eddie, talking to him and cradling one of Eddie's hands, which was now missing two fingers, with both of his hands. Tony removed his jacket and wrapped it tightly around Eddie's hand to help stop the blood flow, but it was useless.

Since the responding officers knew Tony, an ambulance was called, and Eddie was taken to the hospital, but was pronounced dead before the ambulance arrived at the emergency entrance.

After this incident, the police shut down the popular nightclub due to racial unrest – or so the newspapers said.

The Williams sisters tearfully remember the noise, the police at the door, the yelling, screaming, and sobbing, and how disturbing that night in 1961 was for Mrs. Williams. The news devastated the entire family and broke Mrs. Williams into pieces.

When questioned, Mrs. Williams said, "Eddie was just like that," she told reporters and police.

"He was a good man, a good husband and father, always wanting to help anyone in need or just smile at someone to make their day better. He loved his music and felt like a star when that club was full. And in all the years I've known him, he never failed to be respectful of women." Mrs. Williams said, trying to stay calm, but her sobs became louder with each word.

"Please find whoever did this to him. What will we do without him?"

Less than two weeks later, with Tony's help, the police caught up to one of the men who brutalized Eddie from tips and eyewitnesses. He told police who the other two were, but had no reason why they did what they did.

"Hey, man, some guy just hired me to do this. I don't know who he was. I only know that he said to bring two other guys, and I'd get paid when the deed was done."

And with no trial, only an appearance before a judge three weeks later, his killers, who reportedly targeted him for bowing, tipping his hat, and touching the hand of a twenty-two-year-old white woman, were let off with a warning and ninety days of community service. No charges were ever brought against them for the murder of Eddie Williams.

TONY ROSSINI 1968

Amidst the rising racial unrest at this time, the club's owner, Tony Rossini, was forced to sell it. He told the patrons he planned to purchase the local diner from the current owner, who was retiring and moving to another state. The diner was farther away from the club district and a few blocks closer to the residential area of town. It was several city blocks away from the nightclub and appeared to be a safer location.

Tony put up signs in the diner's front window saying he was reopening it as Tony's Family Diner, and everyone was welcome. Anyone thirteen and older could apply to work there.

Since this horrific event, Mrs. Williams's neighbors have helped her family. Cooking for the girls and helping them get to and from their schools and jobs.

Mrs. Williams still worked in the typing pool and began making a name for herself. She became increasingly active in civil rights while taking good care of her daughters and being a good neighbor to all those who helped her so much.

The family was loved without question. Tony always offered them meals from the diner and helped by hiring the daughters when they turned thirteen and fourteen to work there.

Eddie had always been the primary source of income before his death. Mrs. Williams was able to receive welfare because she was a widowed mother. She worked hard not to let welfare become a staple means of living, and she wanted to teach her daughters that they could make a living without it. She taught her daughters ways to save money and get by while building a future.

She took in laundry, cooking, sewing, and babysitting for friends and neighbors to help bring more money into the household. Mrs. Williams was unsure of what the future would bring, but she kept working the domestic jobs from home and worked two or three days a week in the typing pool.

She raised her daughters to be strong and independent while saving as much as possible to escape this mess. Denice and Maymie helped, too, since they both had jobs at Tony's Diner.

Rose couldn't wait to turn thirteen so she could help, too. She was asked to babysit and help clean for a few neighbors, which was a big step for her. She saved every dime.

In 1969, Rose was fourteen, almost fifteen. She went to the diner to ask about a job.

Tony asked Rose, "How old are you now, Rose?"

"Old enough to work here, I think, Mr. Tony. I'll be fifteen in a few months!" Rose declared.

"Hmmm, OK, Rose, I can use your help," said Tony.

He gave Rose a job as soon as she asked. He had known the family well for many years, ever since the girls were babies, and wanted to help them as much as possible after what had happened to Eddie.

Rose was intelligent, attractive, and well-spoken. She had a unique way of making people feel comfortable around her. She listened and was always interested in what anyone had to say.

Tony said, "Rose, I think you'll do well waiting tables and interacting with the customers. You can learn the ropes from Stella, our head waitress."

Rose was thrilled and excited to get the job. "When can I start, Mr. Tony?" asked Rose jubilantly.

"Let's get you started tomorrow after school if your mom approves. You can learn from Stella and start earning tips while you're learning. Your pay will be the same as your sisters', except you will get tips from waiting tables and helping Stella at the counter in addition to the hourly wage of one dollar."

To Rose, one dollar an hour was big money for a teenager. She was elated as she spun around and said, "Oh, thank you so much, Mr. Tony! I won't let you down."

Tony smiled and shook hands with Rose, "See you tomorrow after school."

She couldn't wait to go home and announce her success to the family.

When she got home, she burst through the door and yelled, "Mama, Denice, Maymie! I got a job at Tony's Diner! I start tomorrow after school!"

Everyone had just finished dinner, and they were beginning to clean the dishes and get June started on her homework.

"Rose, I am so proud of you," said Mrs. Williams as she embraced her daughter and said, "Sit down, and I'll get you some dinner so you can tell us more."

June, who was twelve, jumped into Rose's arms, "Oh, Rose!"

The other sisters all came in for a group hug. Denice turned on the radio, and they all danced and sang, "Let the sun shine, Let the sun shine in," dancing and spinning around until they dropped.

"OK, girls, finish your homework and get ready for bed. Tomorrow is a big day for Rose," Mrs. Williams announced.

LILY and ALICE 1968

During her Freshman year, Lily met Alice Russell, a tall blonde girl in her class. When they met in Algebra class, Lily knew something was different. Alice had chin-length, sometimes unruly, wavy blonde hair cut into a pageboy that she sometimes tamed with a headband. She had compelling hazel eyes with dark brown flecks, and a beautiful smile. She wore clear lavender-framed glasses that sat perfectly on her thin nose, which was a little long, but looked beautiful.

Alice was a little taller than Lily and always wore sneakers to school. The dress code stated that girls had to wear dresses that hit the top of the knees or just below the knee, but it didn't specify what kind of shoes.

She had noticed Alice in class before, but never had the courage to talk to her, even though Alice always smiled and waved to her. She was always shy around new people and kids who she wanted to like her and not notice her birthmark. Today was different. She felt brave enough to approach Alice.

After class on a typical Tuesday, Lily bashfully asked Alice, "Would you like to meet my best friends and have lunch together?"

Alice was shy but told Lily, "Yes, that would be great."

On the way to the lunch room, Lily felt a shower of butterflies in her stomach. It was completely different from anything she had ever experienced. She didn't understand what it meant, but couldn't wait to introduce Iris and Rose to Alice.

As Lily approached their usual lunch table with Alice, Lily walked over to the flower girls and introduced Alice. Iris and Rose smiled and were happy to meet her.

"Hi guys, this is Alice. She's in my algebra class," Lily stated happily.

"Hi, Alice," Iris said, "You're on the basketball team, right?"

"Yes, I am!" replied Alice.

"Nice to meet you," said Rose.

Seeing that Lily was so taken with Alice, Iris and Rose looked at each other and exchanged approving smiles.

"We've been talking about what to do after graduation and what direction our lives will take," said Rose.

"Yes", said Lily. "I am planning to travel and become a journalist and reporter. Maybe a photographer for the news, too. Have you thought about what you want to do, Alice?"

"I have", said Alice. "I was hoping to go on to college sports, but I'm not in the running for a basketball scholarship. I'm considering medical school or possibly work as an EMT and rescue medic, and maybe even a firefighter, if they allow women to apply."

"Oh my gosh, that's amazing," said Rose.

All three flower girls were impressed with Alice's goals.

The girls were elated and talkative all through lunch. When the bell rang to signal the end of lunch, Lily asked Alice, "Alice, would you like to get together sometime after school or on the weekend to study?"

"Thanks, Lily. Yes, that would be great." They both smiled as they turned to go to separate classes.

At the end of the school day, the Flower Girls gathered to wait for the buses.

Iris said, "Lily, Alice is so nice! We all like her a lot."

Lily replied, "She is very nice. I want to talk to you guys because I think I have feelings for her. I mean, romantic-type feelings. What does that mean? Is it OK?"

Rose said, "It means just that. You like her as more than a friend. And that is OK and very cool!"

"We've all talked about crushes and boys we've gone out with, and this is no different," said Iris. "I remember when you had a little crush on my brother, Max." Iris giggled.

"This feels different," said Lily, blushing.

THE WILLIAMS SISTERS 1969

Denice and her husband, Gerald Brown, worked to help the family financially. As a teenager, Denice worked at the diner but moved to a better part-time job in the secretarial pool where her mother worked.

Gerald worked at a meat packing plant and helped distribute Chicago's African-American newspaper, the Chicago Defender. The two were a happy, industrious couple who put family first, as they had been taught. Pearl was born in 1967 when Denice was eighteen years old. Pearl was lovingly doted on as the first grandchild. The little family lived in the house with the rest of the Williams family. The sisters all helped with the children and the finances.

Maymie lived with her son, Clay, and Clay's father, Jimmy Barnes. Clay was born just a year after Pearl when Maymie was sixteen. The house bustled with excitement and joy during the holidays and summers. It was a full house and becoming even more crowded, and the family loved each other without question.

Maymie left her job at the diner when she became pregnant with Clay. Jimmy brought in good pay, but at the time, no one knew what he did to earn the money he brought home.

Maymie worked at Tony's diner from age thirteen until she became pregnant with Clay. Then, she worked for the neighbors, babysitting, doing laundry, dog walking, and doing other small jobs she could while pregnant. When Clay was born, Jimmy told her she didn't have to work. She argued with him, saying her contribution to the family was significant, and she wanted to keep working.

When she had recovered from Clay's birth and felt secure leaving him alone with her mom and sisters, Maymie worked on Saturdays for a few hours at the typing pool. She cleaned for friends and neighbors for decent pay. That meant she could still be close enough to come home when needed and busy enough to feel like she was significantly working to have a hand in supporting the family. She also worked on Saturdays for a few hours at Tony's.

JUNE WILLIAMS 1969

June was the youngest in the Williams family, born in 1957, two and a half years behind Rose. At twelve, she was a tiny beauty with soft, golden amber eyes like Rose and her mama. She had dimples and an enormous smile that melted hearts. Sometimes, people would turn and gaze at June because she glowed and was so beautiful. She was the smallest of the Williams sisters but very strong in mind and body, and would always say what she was thinking.

She was wiry, a fast runner like her sister Rose, and could climb, hang, and swing for hours on the monkey bars at the playground. She loved her hair in twists or plaits with colorful bows and barrettes. Her favorite color was bright neon yellow. June was forever happy, singing and dancing around. She loved her sisters' records by Johnny Mathis, Smokey Robinson (her favorite), Sam Cooke, Marvin Gaye, Little Richard, and The Supremes.

June seemed to float and dance through the air instead of walking or running as she sang at the top of her lungs, "Oh, I heard it through the grapevine, oh I'm just about to lose my mind…" and "Stop! In the Name of Love," holding one hand out like a stop sign with her feet wide, and the other hand on her hip as she sang. The Williams sisters would giggle and sing along with June as they joined hands in a circle to dance and pretend they were on American Bandstand. "Sing it, Junie," they would say.

Rose and June were best friends as well as sisters since they were so close in age.

On a typical warm Saturday morning in May, June asked, "Rose, will you take me to the diner with you so I can get a strawberry shake?" June did this hard-to-resist thing of clasping her little hands under her chin and blinking her big, beautiful eyes.

"Please...I can walk there since you have to go to work early, and you could walk home with me."

Rose replied sweetly, "Oh, Junie, you know I have to go to work now and then finish my math homework, and I don't think Mama would like you to walk there alone. But let's see if Denice or Maymie can take you."

June called her big sisters to ask if one of them would take her to the diner.

"I can't, Junie. I am working late today," said Denice.

Maymie walked over to June, knelt down, gently laying her hands on Junie's shoulders, and said, "I have to work at the typing pool today since it's Saturday. But I bet Jimmy can take you for your shake. Mama will be here to take care of Clay and Pearl. But you tell Jimmy that you have to come straight back home after to help Mama with the kids and dinner."

"OK!" June said excitedly.

Maymie called for Jimmy, who was on the phone, speaking quietly with whoever was on the other end. "Jimmy, can you come into the living room for a minute?"

Jimmy replied, "Yeah, be right there." His voice lowered as he said, "Yeah, I'll be there." Jimmy hung the phone back in the cradle on the kitchen wall.

June loved Jimmy. He was always kind and listened to her like she was important and more of an adult than a little kid, and he was always willing to help her with schoolwork.

"Uncle Jimmy, can we PLEASE go to the diner for a strawberry milkshake this afternoon?" June asked, again, her hands clasped tightly under her chin, and that great big, dimply smile and big eyes.

Jimmy said, "Sure thing, little Honey. Is it Saturday already?"

Jimmy loved June like a little sister. His nickname for her was Honey, and he always kept a close eye on her whenever they went anywhere together. Saturdays were their day to do something fun.

"YAY! Thanks, Uncle Jimmy! I can't wait!" Cheered June. "Mama, is that OK?"

Mrs. Williams smiled at the two and agreed that the outing was fine. Then she returned to the kitchen, saying, "Now, Jimmy, you watch out for our little Junie bug!"

"I won't let her out of my sight," Jimmy promised.

Jimmy and June left around noon, holding hands and talking. June laughed and skipped to keep up with Jimmy's long legs on the way to Tony's. The two went into Tony's Diner and sat down at the counter. June could see Tony in the kitchen and waved to Rose, who was waiting on customers at a booth.

"Hello, Mr. Tony!" June said, waving to Tony and smiling that stunning, hard-to-resist smile.

"Looks like you're here for your favorite treat, a special strawberry shake, June bug. Well, today I will personally make it just for you with extra strawberries on top, and how about a little whipped cream?" said Tony.

June blushed and covered her mouth with her tiny, smooth hands to catch the "OOOO" and little squeal that escaped from her voice. She had known Tony all her life and thought he was just like a movie star since he was bigger than life and everybody knew him.

Tony said, "It's on the house, little lady." He winked at Jimmy, who smiled and nodded back. Lots of chatter and giggles ensued.

When it was time to head back home, Jimmy said, "Let's go, Junie. I have some things I have to do later today."

"OK, Uncle Jimmy, thank you for the treat, and thanks, Mr. Tony!" June announced, wearing pink dabs of strawberries and ice cream on her nose, cheeks, and down the front of her lime green t-shirt with neon yellow sunflowers on the front.

"This was fun! I wish we could come here every day," said June.

Jimmy said, "Me too, Honey, me too."

The two walked towards the front door and waved to Tony. Jimmy turned to nod to Tony and saw a man sitting alone in the back booth of the diner who got up to leave out of the diner's back door. He looked familiar, but Jimmy didn't think much about it.

As they reached the sidewalk in front of Tony's, Jimmy said, "Honey, I am going to let you walk home by yourself today while I watch to be sure you get back safe."

June asked, "Is that OK? I never did that before, but I know the way."

Jimmy said, "Good, I know you will be OK since I'll be watching. When you get to the corner, do you know which direction to turn to get to our house?"

June said, "Yes, I turn left," holding up her left hand, " and our house is just three houses on the right across the street."

Yes," said Jimmy. "You are getting so grown up, Junie. Don't forget to look both ways before you cross the street to our house, OK? I'm so proud of you. Now you know that I will be watching. You can turn around anytime, and I will be there. Wave to me when you are ready to cross the street."

"OK, Uncle Jimmy," said June, skipping down the sidewalk.

Jimmy watched every step she took to be sure she was safely on her way. June turned to wave to Jimmy twice: once when she was ready to turn the corner and once more as she turned, then disappeared to cross the street. He felt a massive sigh of relief, not realizing he had been holding his breath as she waved to him to show that she was OK.

Just as Jimmy turned to go back to the diner's front door, a silver-gray armored truck sped past him, followed by a police car. He'd seen trucks like this at the bank. He turned quickly, "What the hell…?"

He watched where the truck went. The tires squealed as the driver flew around the corner where June was crossing the street. The police car was following closely. Jimmy saw the driver of the truck through the side window but didn't recognize him. He didn't notice any other windows except the windshield. He saw what appeared to be letters or a logo blacked out on the side and back of the truck.

"Man, this is not good," Jimmy said quietly. He felt a bolt of lightning strike from the inside…"Junie! I know you're okay. I know you got home." He thought, "What if she was crossing the street, and that truck hit her?"

Jimmy shuddered. "No way, I know she's home now. I would have heard something."

But everything in him didn't honestly believe that she was OK. Jimmy didn't hear anything but tires screeching as they rounded the corner.

With his head down, Jimmy mumbled, "Junie, I know you're OK. I'll see you in a few days."

Jimmy felt rattled but knew he had to go. He looked through the diner's big front window and noticed it was still packed with customers who wanted to sit in the air conditioning, have lunch, and have a cool drink.

As he walked around to the back of the diner, Jimmy thought he had recognized the man at the back booth, who looked straight at him earlier, but he had let it slide from his memory. The man was gone, and besides, other things were more important. Then he went behind the building to the alley, into the diner's backdoor, and down the kitchen stairs.

MAX 1969

In the Spring of his junior year, Iris's brother, Max, had his eyes fixed on a stunning dark-haired girl standing at her locker, surrounded by her friends. When the friends walked away to go to their classes, Max approached this beautiful girl and introduced himself.

"M-m-my name is Max. I saw you at your locker. Are you new here?"

She looked up at him and smiled. "My name is Selena, and I've been at this school for three years."

"Oh, I haven't seen you before. But I'm glad I did today," said Max, turning red with embarrassment.

Selena, with her long, thick, dark, slightly wavy hair and deep brown eyes with eyelashes so long that when she blinked, it looked like butterflies fluttering on her soft tan cheekbones, grinned and said,

"Well, I don't make it to school every day."

The two teens walked together down the hall, and Max felt sparks fly.

"Selena," said Max, "Your name is beautiful. You are beautiful." Then Max felt like liquid inside and had a sinking feeling in his stomach, thinking those words sounded dumb.

"It means moon," said Selena, "My name means moon."

Max had never felt this way with a girl before. It was overwhelming. His brain felt like mush, and his body suddenly became floppy like the bunny ears of Iris's old, worn-out stuffed rabbit.

He could hear Iris in his thoughts saying in a singsong voice, "Max is in looove!" It made him smile and feel sort of freaky at the same time. "Could I walk home with you after school?" asked Max.

Selena said, "OK, but only until we get to my corner." Max grinned and nodded.

After that, Max started each day by meeting Selena outside her locker before their classes and at lunchtime. He always offered to carry her books as they walked home from school together. Selena and Max talked about school, their friends, and nothing and everything. They would walk as far as they could until they had to split off to head home.

Selena always broke away first. "OK, Max, this is where I have to go a different way." Max figured she must live in the opposite direction, but Selena didn't want her brother to see her with Max.

"See you tomorrow," said Max with a goofy teenage lovestruck grin.

At home, Iris teased, "Max has a girlfriend," as she danced in circles around him. Max turned as red as a ripe apple.

Mrs. O'Brien asked, "So, Max, who is this girlfriend?" She was happy that he had found someone he really liked. "What's her name?"

"Mom, please!" said Max in a drawn-out, embarrassed tone.

"Just asking," said Mrs. O'Brien with a grin.

Max said, "Selena, her name is Selena. Oh, Mom, she is so

beautiful and funny, and she likes me too".

Mrs. O'Brien smiled at her beaming son. "Would you like to invite her to dinner, Max?"

"I would, but I don't know if...OK, I'll see if she can come. Thanks, Mom."

Max was a little apprehensive since he had never met Selena's family, except for her brother, Sebastian, once at school. He was very cautious about Sebastian, who was a year older and had dropped out of school. Max saw the guys Sebastian hung out with, but they were not the guys he wanted to hang out with.

Spring moved quickly, leading Max and Selena to discuss their summer plans. "I'm planning to work over the summer and save money to buy a car," said Max.

Selena replied, "I have no plans right now. This year has not been so good at home," said Selena. "My parents are so stressed all the time and arguing constantly, I think they might be ready to split up."

Max asked, "Why didn't you tell me? Can I help?"

Selena said, "I can't keep up with school assignments, and my friends are so distant. I feel like I'm on the verge of tears at least once a day. You're the only thing that makes me happy, Max."

Max put his arm around her shoulder as they approached the shiny wooden bench in the park on their way home.

Selena continued, "My brother is never home like he used to be, and I don't want to talk to him anyway. His hoodlum friends are awful, and they're always around. He only talks to me when he's telling me what to do, you know, bossing me around. Max, you seem like my only salvation.”

As they sat together hand in hand at the end of this school day on this sunny, warm Thursday afternoon, Selena asked, “Max, will you run away with me?”

Max was startled and caught off guard. “Selena, I can't run away. I want to graduate and go to college. My parents would freak out if I ran off.”

Selena told him, “Fine, I will run away anyway. I can't stand Sebastian controlling my life, and his friends scare me. I will find a way to go South, to my Uncle's place in Texas, where it's always warm, away from here, even if I have to hitchhike. My parents won't care. They won't even miss me.”

Max pleaded with her not to go, “Selena, don't go, don't run! It's so dangerous out there alone. You know what's been on the news. You're only fifteen years old, Selena.”

“Look, Max,” Selena said, showing a strong will of her own, “I am going to be just fine, with or without you.”

She walked away, raising her hand to stop Max from talking or following her, and didn't even turn around to look at him.

With his head down, Max said, “Selena, I think I love you. Please don't go.”

She kept walking. Then he stood up and called to her, “WAIT! Meet me at the lighted picnic table in this park tonight, a little after dark.”

Selena turned to look at Max, nodded, and turned the other way.

Selena went home. She slipped quietly into the house and went to her bedroom. She pulled her long dark hair into a ponytail, gathered a few things, including a folded map from the gas station, the money she had saved from babysitting in the neighborhood, and a few things from her dresser, and put them into a tan leather sling bag.

When it was just about dark, she tossed the bag out of her bedroom window and quietly slipped out of the same window, jumping to the lawn below.

"I have no idea where to go except South. I'm so tired of cold weather six months out of the year. I can always be warm and away from Sebastian and his gang. And away from my parents. Max is the only person I trust," she said quietly so no one would hear her out on the lawn.

Max went home and told his mom, "Mom, I'm going out after dinner to meet some friends."

He didn't tell her where or what time. She wasn't concerned since Max was always a good kid. He was never in trouble, studied hard, made good grades, and kept a close watch on Iris.

"Max, have you asked Selena if she would like to join us this Saturday for dinner?" said Mrs. O'Brien.

Max said, "Not yet. I'll ask her later, I promise." Mrs. O'Brien smiled and nodded.

After dinner, Mrs. O'Brien noticed that Max didn't eat much. She thought he appeared nervous but believed he was just apprehensive about asking Selena to dinner. Max was so shy.

Just after dinner, when the sun went down and the sky was a transparent shade of Lapis, not yet the usual darker midnight blue, Max left for the park to meet Selena. It was just a few blocks in the direction of the school. He waited at the picnic table for what seemed like an eternity. His knees bounced nervously, and his palms were dry and sweaty at the same time as they pressed into his knees.

Once he saw Selena, he waved her over. "Selena, over here," he said quietly. She nodded her head cautiously and looked over her shoulder.

Then Max spotted someone behind her hiding between the trees. "Oh man, what is this?" asked Max.

It was Sebastian. He had followed Selena, suspicious that she was out after dark to meet up with Max.

Sebastian got closer, grabbed Selena's arm, and pulled her back to his chest, moving his arm around her neck and shoulders.

"Hello, Max, what are you doing here?" Sebastian asked in an accusing tone.

Max answered, "Nothing – just talking with your sister about a school project."

Selena pleaded with Sebastian, "Sebastian, what are you doing? Let me GO!" That made him yank her back with more force.

Then Max stood up. He was taller, muscular, and bigger than Sebastian. He was an athlete. He asked Sebastian, "What's the problem here?"

Sebastian turned his head to look behind him, only to see some of his fellow gang members there.

That sight made Sebastian stand tall and puff his chest like an alpha hairy ape. "I told you—you better leave my sister alone. She doesn't want a guy like you," said Sebastian with pseudo confidence.

Selena twisted herself out of Sebastian's grip and stood between the two teenagers, one arm spread in each direction, hands out.

Max and Selena became anxious and a little spooked.

Selena yelled at Sebastian, "This needs to stop right now! You cannot control my life, Sebastian! I will not take this. You and your nasty club boys better leave me alone. I will see Max if I want to. He is not like you. He cares about the future, and he cares about me. He is not like you, big brother! Stop chasing away every boy I like!"

Just then, a police car patrolling the park noticed the encounter. The car stopped, and the officer driving rolled down his window and asked, "Is there any trouble here?"

Sebastian, who had let go of his sister, quickly said, "No" to the officer.

The black officer said, "I'm Officer Robinson. You kids all need to go home before you get into big trouble. Unless you want to take a ride down to the station with me. I recognize you and your group of troublemakers, Sebastian. There will be no trouble tonight, got it? Now go home, all of you!"

The teens nodded their heads and slowly started to leave. Sebastian looked back at Max with laser-point eyes that could pierce the dark and leave marks. Max stared at him intensely, then at Selena.

"I'm going home, and we'll talk tomorrow, Selena," he said.

Officer Robinson waited and watched closely as the kids all scattered in different directions. Max made a mental note to remember the officer's name and said to himself, "Officer Robinson."

When Max got home, he immediately went to his room and wrote down the officer's name. As he ran back down the stairs, his mom greeted him.

"How did it go when you asked Selena about dinner?"

Max said, "I didn't ask her yet. Her brother was there with some of his friends." We all left the park before I could speak to her.

Mrs. O'Brien noticed that Max was shaken and nervous. She told Max, "That's OK, you can ask her anytime, like at school tomorrow."

The next day was Friday. Max and Iris got up and got ready for school at a sluggish Friday pace.

Mr. O'Brien shouted upstairs, "Kids, I am driving you to school this morning, but you will need to take the bus home."

Max nodded in silence.

"And Max, stay with your sister. Iris, stay with Max, I mean it."

"OK, Daddy", said Iris.

"I will, Dad," said Max.

IRIS 1969

As the Vietnam War escalated, the boys in school who planned to go to college and were accepted as full-time students were exempt from the draft lottery. Men aged eighteen through twenty-six were legally required to register for the draft. Most boys in school were under that age, but it was unnerving to everyone, nonetheless.

"What if Max was older?" thought Iris. That thought made her shudder.

Iris had a classmate and friend, Jeannie, whose boyfriend had graduated from high school in 1968 and had not registered for any colleges or universities because he had a good job with his dad's grocery company.

Glen was selected in the draft lottery the day after his eighteenth birthday. Jeannie was frightened and proud of him all at the same time. He was to leave for training camp as an air patrol pilot, providing aerial support to ground troops in South Vietnam and airlift operations, piloting a transport aircraft to move personnel and supplies throughout the region. He was excited about this and could see a future as a pilot.

Jeannie was a little older, a junior at their high school. She was a friend who needed support, and Iris was there for her.

Glen was to leave in the fall of 1970, just at the beginning of Jeannie's senior year. She confided to Iris that they were getting married in July before he had to leave.

The Flower Girls helped Jeannie work through her family's

feelings about all of this confusion. Her family was so concerned that the two getting married was not the right thing for Jeannie, but it did not stop her from marrying her boyfriend before he left.

They had a courthouse wedding, and the parents were there. The Flower Girls held a small reception at Jeannie's house with the help of their moms. Jeannie and her new husband, Glen, were happy and looked forward to their future together when he could return.

Glen's bus left on September 14th. His parents were there, along with Jeannie's parents and so many other families going through the same emotions.

Jeannie kissed him. "Oh, Glen, why is this happening? I love you."

Glen put his arms around her shoulders and looked into her eyes. "Jeannie, I love you, and I will be back so we can start our lives together. I promise. Write me every day." Tears welled up in Glen's eyes as Jeannie wrapped her arms tightly around him.

He tried his best to hide his red eyes and tears, not wanting to let the other families and recruits see. To his surprise, most of the young men there were in a world of tears and fear. He was not alone.

His parents held Glen for what felt like hours as his father had to help his mother let go of him. Her hands moved to Glen's face as she tried to compose herself for her son.

"Glen, we love you and will write to you every week."

"Godspeed, son," said Glen's father as he shook his hand in pride and ever-present concern.

Then, in what felt like a millisecond, Glen and the other soldiers were herded and loaded onto the bus. Distressed tears flowed from every distraught person watching. It would have been enough to fill a river.

Glen waved to Jeannie and blew her a kiss and a nod with a nervous, unsettled smile. He was just as terrified as she was, even more so, but never wanted her to see it. He wanted Jeannie and his parents to see his bravery.

Before leaving the bus station to go home and waving continuously to the new servicemen whose noses and hands were still pressed against the bus windows, their families and loved ones watched, maybe for the last time.

Jeannie had a haunting, fearsome rush of electricity encasing and striking her. Every hair on her entire body stood up as she shivered like it was the dead of winter. She was ghostly pale as she looked at her mother and said, "I don't think I'll ever see him again."

"Oh, Jeannie, we have to have faith that he'll return safely." Her mother held her tight as they wept together, using all the tears they had inside and then some.

As the school year progressed, Iris and the other flower girls stayed close to Jeannie.

"Glen has been writing letters to me as often as he can. He says that he misses me terribly and that he misses my smile, my silly laugh, and my big hugs. He can't wait to start our life together when he comes home. And neither can I," said Jeannie

Jeannie told the Flower Girls. "I write to him every day, and my mom mails them for me. I get letters from Glen occasionally, whenever he can get them mailed."

"Do you know what he does over there exactly ?" Iris asked sincerely.

Jeannie said, "He wrote that he is providing aerial support to ground troops in South Vietnam and learning airlift operations to move personnel and supplies throughout the region. That's the version he wrote to me. I don't understand everything, but it's brave and powerful. I'm so proud of him. He decided he wants to be a pilot when he comes home."

"Wow," said Iris. "It sounds so important and scary. He's so brave!"

Lily said, "I finally found out what my father does. It has to do with the war. He never talked about it, and I just decided to ask him since everything is so terribly mysterious. He told me that he develops chemicals for warfare. It's supposed to help us win this war, but I think it's more harmful and deadly in the long run. I pray it doesn't hurt Glen and the troops."

Jeannie said, "I'm just so frightened and nervous."

Lily replied, "We all are, and we'll keep praying."

"Group hug!" Rose shouted with outstretched arms.

Jeannie spoke to Iris alone, "Iris, I just cannot shake this feeling of dread and doom. I miss Glen so much, and I am so terrified and uneasy. I can't concentrate on anything else."

Iris said, "I think I know how to help, at least temporarily."

Iris and the other flower girls planned a shopping trip and a movie to distract Jeannie from her stressful situation.

"Let's go to the mall for a little window shopping and catch a movie. That will take your mind off things for an afternoon," Iris said to Jeannie.

On their Saturday shopping and movie trip, they bought matching bracelets and hats and had a whale of a time together. They went to see Cactus Flower because they all loved Goldie Hawn. None of them was in the mood to see M.A.S.H. or Love Story. Something funny was the ticket right now.

After a wonderful day of laughter, friendship, secrets, and time to breathe, they all headed to the park bench where Max was picking them all up to go home for time with their families and a good night's sleep, which was hard for Jeannie to come by.

Eight months later, almost to the day that Glen left, a courier notified Jeannie and Glen's parents. Jeannie's father answered the door, and the courier placed an official letter in his hand.

"Dad, I want to open it," said Jeannie.

"Are you sure, sweetheart?" He asked.

"Yes, Dad, I need to do this." He gently gave her the envelope.

She read it aloud.

"We regret to inform you that Airman Pilot Glen Walker's plane exploded in air sabotage while on an airlift supply mission. All personnel onboard perished. Be proud of his brave and heroic actions. He was a hero to all during this unsettling time.

His belongings will be forwarded to you, his parents, and his wife. His body will be sent to you with the highest honors. Once again, we send you our deepest condolences for your loss. Thank you, Colonel James F. Murphy, USAF.”

“I can't read anymore,” said Jeannie. She fell to the floor on her knees as the letter silently floated from her hand. Her body convulsed uncontrollably with heavy sobs as she buried her head in her hands.

“Jeannie, I'm here,” said her mother, getting on the floor and pulling her tightly to her chest. She kissed her forehead and stroked her smooth chestnut-brown hair.

Jeannie's worst fears had come true, and she was utterly broken and devastated, unable to finish the school semester.

A few days later, her mother told Iris, “Jeannie is in the hospital for a while.”

“Can we see her or bring her flowers?” asked Iris.

“Maybe you girls should wait. She isn't speaking to anyone and stares off into the distance most of the time. Her doctor and counselors tell us she will get better.”

“Oh no, I’m so sad about this. We'll get her a card and have everyone sign it so you can give it to her when she's ready,” Iris replied.

“Thank you, Iris, you’re a good friend. You know, they call her Mrs. Walker in the hospital. It feels strange,” said Jeannie’s mother.

When Jeannie was discharged from the hospital, the Flower Girls visited her at home. They would knock on the door every other day. Her mother would answer and tell them if it was a good day or not. Sometimes, it was.

Two weeks from the last visit, Jeannie's mother called Iris, "Iris, we are getting Jeannie and Glen's marriage annulled. The psychologist says this will help her move forward in her life. We are also working with the therapists to decide what will help her most."

"Thank you for letting me know. I love Jeannie and only want the best for the rest of her life," said Iris.

Eventually, Jeannie left home to live with her Aunt in Iowa.

Iris, Rose, and Lily stayed in touch with her by phone until she stopped returning their calls.

Her Aunt told them she couldn't move on until she could process everything that had happened. "She may contact you later, but it has to be her decision. Thanks to all of you girls for being there unconditionally for Jeannie. She loves you and will never forget your compassion and kindness."

Iris, Lily, and Rose held on to each other, and with heartfelt wishes to Jeannie, they cried and prayed together that she would recover and find true love in her life again.

Iris never stopped sending her letters and Christmas cards.

That summer, Iris began to make concrete plans for college and beyond. She would pursue a Master's degree in Social Work. She was full-on ready to work with community organizing and groups to address local issues related to the matters Rose's family faced throughout their years as best friends, such as poverty, violence, housing, and healthcare disparities. She would also address racial discrimination and advocate for equal access to housing, education, and employment opportunities. Her experience with Rose and the Williams family fueled her ambition.

After what happened with Jeannie, Iris also became involved in anti-Vietnam War activism, working to support returning veterans and advocate against the war's impacts on communities and families.

"I want to make a difference in this messed-up world. We have to do better," she said in a spring speech to her classmates.

LILY 1969

"Can you believe we will start high school after summer?" Lily said, sounding more grown-up. The girls talked about what they wanted to do after high school when they entered college.

Lily exclaimed, "I always thought of myself as just another American kid like everyone else since I grew up in America from the time I was just a child."

She said, "My parents always stressed that to me, but it was always understood that I had to be better than the other American kids. You know, do better in school, art, and sports."

Lily continued, "I like my science and math classes, but I honestly want to become a journalist, like we see on TV. I want to go places, interview important people all over the world, and write for magazines and newspapers. I wish my parents would listen to me when I tell them I want to do this. They want me to be a scientist like my father. Now that I know my father is involved in chemical engineering, making weird gases and sprays for the war, I feel the need to report about the dangers to the public. I heard my mom tell my dad that the things he works on are potentially very hazardous and dangerous."

Rose asked, "Why? What is it?"

Lily replied, "I never spoke to him about it until now, but since I'm a little older, I see things on the news and remember what Jeannie told us. Even though he believes it is wrong to make these chemical agents, he works under contract for the company and must follow their directives. He doesn't want me involved in anything unsafe or deadly. But I want... no, I NEED, to know the real news, the real truth of things happening here and worldwide, and report it so people will know that truth."

She continued, "I want to make a difference by bringing the news and truth to the people about the war, politics, and everything that goes with it. I plan to take a photography class so I can write and journal with photos. And what if the chemical agents he makes hurt him after all these years?"

She added, "The only thing that bothers me about working in this field is if my birthmark will hold me back. People are not always very tolerant."

Iris said, "Don't worry about your birthmark, Lily. If you're nervous about it, wear scarves. You are so beautiful that no one will even notice. I can see you doing all of that. You're going to be a great journalist and reporter. Maybe the next Barbara Walters!"

Lily said, "Thanks, Iris. I take notes of even the most unimportant-looking things whenever I read newspapers and watch television news and reports. I write down everything because I don't want to miss something that could be significant."

Iris continued, "I plan to attend college to become a social worker. Helping people who don't have enough to get what they need to live a better life. It feels right to me. I want to be the one to help them advance in their lives and be able to care for their families. Finding ways to give them a chance at a better job or even to start their own business. If I can help orphaned children or kids in foster care find forever families, that would fill my heart.”

Rose put her hands to her cheeks and said to Iris, “Thank you, Iris. My family needs someone like you, so do many people in this city. And Lily, bringing truth and news to the people is brave and necessary, and I know you will be amazing at it. You two are so full of courage and hope.”

“Rose, what do you want to do?” Said Lily.

Rose said, “I decided a long time ago that I am going to law school to learn the judicial system and how the government works, like we’ve been learning about in our social studies and government classes. I want to understand how the courts work and how the law can be fair. Bringing people to justice like those who killed my daddy and to make life safer for people like my family.”

“Now, who’s the brave one?” said Iris, forming her hands into a crown over Rose’s head.

Iris, Rose, and Lily cheered, pumped their hands in the sky, and gave each other a standing ovation.

“We all have such big, bold ideas for the future. Let’s make them happen.” Said Lily.

THE WILLIAMS FAMILY May 10th 1969

Rose's family helped her save from their earnings, and she was allowed to save all of hers for college and law school tuition. Mrs. Williams, with Tony's help, opened a college savings account for Rose at the bank. She could make deposits each week and watch it grow.

By the spring of 1969, Mrs. Williams moved her family out of Woodlawn to a slightly larger home in the Chatham neighborhood. At that time, parts of the Southside seemed to be growing, as was the Williams family.

She considered moving the family to the black section on the Northside, but could not afford the cost or get a loan. They settled in Chatham and started what they hoped would be a better life.

The home was nicer than the previous apartment, with a tiny postage stamp-sized yard in the back with a fence, and an even smaller yard in front. The sisters were overjoyed. Mrs. Williams picked up one more day a week at her typing pool job since the girls were older and more responsible. This was working out just fine.

Rose, Iris, and Lily would graduate from high school in just two years. Although they attended the same school, they were no longer segregated in classes. The Flower Girls' families knew each other and loved each other's company, and how comfortable and safe they were in that friendship.

The girls were allowed to walk around in safe areas of town for window shopping or go to the diner together. They could attend movies together if one of the parents drove them and picked them up. The families started getting more involved and trusted each other without question to be part of their children's lives and each other's lives, and this, in turn, saw The Flower Girls becoming closer as they grew, learning from their big, extended, diverse family.

Rose's two older sisters graduated from high school. That was the promise they made to their mother. June, or Junie, as she was affectionately called, the youngest, was two and a half years younger than Rose and always looked up to her. Denice and Maymie worked at Tony's Diner throughout high school and didn't attend college, even though Mrs. Williams hoped they would focus on careers. She was proud of each one of them, nonetheless.

Both Denice and Maymie had young children. Denice married a hard-working man, Gerald Brown, and had a daughter, Pearl, named after Mrs. Williams. Maymie had a son, Clay, who was younger than Pearl, and lived in the home with her baby's father, Jimmy, but she was not married to him. Jimmy was a decent father, and June loved him,

Maymie felt something wasn't right in Jimmy's work life. She didn't know precisely what he did to bring money into the family, and it worried her that it could be dangerous. Maymie often wondered how to ask him why he was gone so much and what he did to earn the money he brought in.

They all still lived in the same home, which was becoming more crowded than ever. Maymie could not bring herself to leave Jimmy once and for all because she loved him. And little Junie loved him like a big brother. Jimmy was so good with Clay and was such a gentle person.

Only once did she tell him her plan to leave. He threatened to take their son and leave her with nothing. That was the only time she saw his angry side. She never saw it again and never brought it up to him again.

Jimmy was generally a kind man, good to Maymie, and a wonderful father to Clay, but he could also be mysterious to the point of distrust. She also knew that drug running was part of what he did to bring money into the home, and she worried that his lifestyle would cause more significant problems for him and possibly for her family. She avoided his dealings without saying a word to anyone, not even her sisters, and never spoke to him about it after the first time.

One very warm, sunny Saturday afternoon in May, around 4:30 p.m., Mrs. Williams asked, "Rose and Denice, have either of you seen Junie today?"

"No, I thought she was with you, Mama," said Rose.

"I haven't seen her since this morning before I went to work," said Denice.

Maymie, who had just returned home from work, overheard the conversation and immediately stepped into the room, carrying her young son, Clay, in her arms. She said, "Jimmy isn't here either. He said that he was going to take Junie to Tony's for a milkshake like they do for fun on some Saturdays, but that was earlier, around noon.

And they are always home by 2 p.m. at the latest."

Rose felt uneasy and frantically said, "I saw them there while I was working, but I left at 1 p.m."

Rose continued, "Mama, we will all go out and look for her, but maybe you should stay home with the babies and wait for Junie if she calls or comes home."

Mrs. Williams nodded in approval while reaching out to Maymie for Clay. She wrapped her strong arms around little Clay and held him closely while calling for Pearl to come to her side.

"I'll be right here. You girls look everywhere you think she might be – even go to the school. Ask everyone if they have seen her – or Jimmy."

"Alright, mama, we'll find her!" said Denice.

MAX AND SELENA May 9th 1969

Selena and Sebastian went home together after the incident in the park. It was late, and Mrs. Ortiz was impatient with the two teens. "Where have you been? Do you know what time it is?"

"Yes, Mami, we do. We were at the park meeting with friends about a school project," said Selena, hoping her mother would take her word for it.

Mrs. Ortiz looked at Sebastian for confirmation. "Um…yes, Ma. We lost track of time."

"Both of you go to bed right now. You have school tomorrow." Mrs. Ortiz was direct and never one to argue with.

With her thick, black, wavy hair styled into a flip that softly brushed the tops of her shoulders and teased at the top of her head, pulled back with a pretty grass green cloth headband, and her wide, deep-set dark brown eyes that sparkled like stars no matter what mood she was in, there was no question that Lucia Ortiz ruled the Ortiz home.

Hector Ortiz always seemed to be working in the neighboring farm fields and missed many events in the lives of the Ortiz kids. Mrs. Ortiz played the roles of disciplinarian, housekeeper, bookkeeper, and taxi driver, keeping the home running smoothly. And she did it impeccably.

This was a contentious issue for Mr. and Mrs. Ortiz, causing them to argue and ignore each other. But they truly loved each other and their children, so they always worked it out, but not always particularly quietly.

Selena and Sebastian looked at each other to confirm that neither would talk more about the night as they turned to go upstairs to their rooms.

"G'night, Mami," said Selena.

"Night, Mom," called Sebastian from the top of the stairs.

Selena closed her bedroom door and put her bag on the bed. By now, it was after 11 p.m., and she had to decide quickly whether to go to bed or take her bag and leave at that very moment.

She decided to lie down for a few minutes. "I'll go before everyone wakes up in the morning," she whispered, looking into her mirror.

Selena fell asleep quickly and was awakened by the sunlight streaming from her window. It was almost 5:30 a.m. Her mom would be in to wake her up to get ready for school in less than one hour. She had to act fast. Selena's mind was made up. She would leave and head South, no matter what. When she got somewhere far enough away, she would call her mom and Max to let them know she was OK.

She silently sneaked into the bathroom to splash water on her face to wake up. She brushed her dark, thick hair, then pulled it back into a ponytail.

Then, tiptoeing back to her bedroom, she checked her bag and counted the money she had stashed in the zipper pocket. There was one ten-dollar bill, one five-dollar bill, seven ones, and some change that she didn't count. She knew it was enough to get a bus ticket to

San Antonio, Texas, and still have a little left for food.

She put on her white and red PF Flyer high-top shoes, pulled her ponytail up and secured it with a clip, put on a black headband, and grabbed her brother's dark blue shiny high school sports jacket.

She put a navy blue scarf over her head to hide her face and cover her hair, then tied it under her chin. Then she threw her bag out the bedroom window again and jumped out as quietly as possible.

Her first stop was Tony's Diner, where she picked up a couple of sandwiches. At this time of day, they were only serving breakfast.

Speaking to Stella at the counter, "May I have two peanut butter sandwiches on Wonderbread, an grape soda, and a glazed doughnut, please."

"Sure, honey," said Stella, "that'll be $2.50."

"Thanks," said Selena, trying to disguise her voice. She stuffed the food into her bag and, with a quick wave to Stella and Tony, she left, trying to appear casual.

"I think they saw who I was, crap. I hope they don't call my mom," mumbled Selena as she hurried down the sidewalk.

Her next stop was the Greyhound bus station, about five blocks west of the diner. She walked as fast as she could, not running, so as not to call attention to herself.

When she got to the bus station, she had to stand in line to get to the counter. The man at the ticket counter looked at her and asked her age.

Selena said, "I'm eighteen." The man asked her for her driver's license.

"Oh, I left it at home since I wasn't going to be driving."

The man said, "Look, kid, I know you aren't eighteen, and I can't sell you a ticket if you're under that age."

Selena stood her ground and told him again, "I AM eighteen."

He was adamant about refusing to sell her a ticket and told her, "Get out of the line unless you can provide proper identification."

Selena turned around. She wasn't scared but disappointed that she hadn't thought of that before she left. If she had known he would ask her, she might have found a way to get her mom's license.

She decided to go outside, wait for the next bus, and try to sneak onboard.

The ticket counter worker saw her sitting on the bench by the wide picture window in front of the bus station, her arms crossed against her chest and her head down. She pushed back her scarf to see better and get some air.

She was gone as quickly as the man looked away to help another customer and then looked out the front window for her again. He had a strange feeling, but thought she had probably just decided to go home. But he was concerned.

When he had cleared all the customers from his ticket line, he called the police station to report that she might be a runaway. He gave the police a description of her and what she was wearing, but didn't know her name. He guessed her age to be about fifteen or sixteen and of Puerto Rican or Mexican descent.

By the time Selena was discovered missing from school, it was almost noon. Max didn't see her in the lunch room, and she wasn't waiting at her locker like usual, so he assumed she was avoiding him.

At the end of the school day, Max decided to go to her house and ask if she had been home that day. When he arrived at the Ortiz home, Sebastian opened the door, almost ready to lunge at Max. "What do you want? What are you doing here?" said Sebastian angrily.

"Whoa," said Max, raising his hands to stop Sebastian, "I was looking for Selena. I didn't see her anywhere at school today. Is she here?"

"What do you mean? I haven't seen her here at home today," shouted Sebastian as he pushed Max backward off the front step.

"Maybe you should tell me where she is," bellowed Sebastian as his face tensed, chin tucked and head reaching forward as if to butt Max in his forehead.

Mrs. Ortiz hurried out of the kitchen and grabbed Sebastian's arm, scolding both boys. "Max, can you tell me first what is going on?"

Max replied in a take-charge tone, "Selena wasn't at school today. I'm worried and don't know where she might be."

Sebastian asked, "Mami, did you see her this morning?"

Max wiped his face with the palms of his hands and asked, "Mrs. Ortiz, may I come in to talk?"

Mrs. Ortiz extended her hand to lead Max into the living room.

"Yes, Max, let's go over everything," she said calmly.

Once inside, all three sat down anxiously. Max announced that he would speak first.

He uneasily explained to Mrs. Ortiz, "Ma'am, yesterday Selena asked me if I would run away with her."

"I knew it!" yelled Sebastian, pounding his fist on his knees.

"If you did anything to her…"

Max spoke up firmly, "I didn't do anything to her. I love her. I told her no. I also told her she shouldn't run away either; it's dangerous, and she's only fifteen."

Mrs. Ortiz put her hands to her eyes, then, squeezing them into fists, tensely dropped them to her lap. "Why, Max? Did she say why?"

Sebastian stood up as if to overpower Max like a gorilla. Mrs. Ortiz told him angrily, "Sit down, Sebastian, right now, and let Max speak." Sebastian heatedly dropped into the burnt orange La-Z-Boy chair, bouncing slightly on the plaid cushion.

"Yes, Mrs. Ortiz," said Max, turning his head towards Sebastian, "She said she was tired of Sebastian bossing her around and controlling her life. She wanted to escape from him and his gang and go somewhere warm. She told me she wanted to go to Texas, where her Uncle lives."

"Sebastian," his mother scolded, "Did you know anything about this?"

Sebastian drooped like a rag doll and spoke quietly, "Yes, Mami, she told me lots of times to leave her alone and stop telling her what to do. I only do that so she will be safe, not to hurt her."

"I'm going to call the police station to report her missing," declared Mrs. Ortiz.

"I suggest you and Max go out and look for her right now and get your hoodlum friends to do the same, Sebastian."

"Mrs. Ortiz," said Max, "when you call, ask for Officer Robinson. He saw us all in the park last night and will help us."

"Thank you, Max, I will ask for him."

Mrs. Ortiz called the police station, "Hello, my name is Lucia Ortiz. I want to report that my daughter, Selena, is missing. I want to speak to Officer Robinson if he is available."

The voice on the other end of the line said, "Yes, he is here." When Officer Robinson came on the line, Mrs. Ortiz fully described Selena.

"Officer Robinson, my daughter Selena's friend, Max, told me you saw them in the park last night and could help. What can we do about this?"

Officer Robinson replied, "I did see the kids and told them to go home. It looked like Sebastian wanted to start something. I'm glad I was there. When did you notice Selena missing, Mrs. Ortiz?"

She replied, "It appears that she never went to school this morning. She is probably wearing her brother's satin high school jacket, a black or dark blue scarf covering her head and eyes, blue jeans, and white P.F. Flyer tennis shoes with a red stripe. She would have been carrying a tan leather sling bag. That's all I noticed missing from her room."

Officer Robinson asked, "Mrs. Ortiz, could you come to the station? Someone working at the bus depot spotted a young girl fitting that description this morning."

"Yes, yes, I will be there as soon as possible," said Mrs. Ortiz.

JUNE WILLIAMS May 12th 1969

The police were not helpful until they discovered June was not the only young person missing over the last three years. There were even more missing reports from years earlier. Several calls and visits to the station by family and friends of missing girls and boys of color, ages twelve through seventeen, were never followed up on, and the calls and visits were put into a file with the drawer closed and locked.

Chief Al Warren was called into the case files room. "Open this drawer marked runaways," he told Officer Robinson, who was on desk duty.

He opened the drawer so Mrs. Williams could see it and pulled out the missing child reports.

Chief Warren was astonished and appalled at how many had never been shared with him by his officers or followed up on. He fell backward into his chair. Looking at Mrs. Williams, her face aghast, he stuttered and stammered, "I-I-I had no idea about what was in these files, ma'am." He said to Mrs. Williams.

Mrs. Williams put her hand over her open mouth and let out a muffled gasp, "What? All of these children, these babies, are missing, and no one has looked for them? If one of these children is a family member of the police force, would it happen the same way?" She was furious.

Each folder was stamped 'RUNAWAY' in bold letters with only the children's names, their parents' names, phone numbers, and addresses. No other information was archived. There was no identification, and only a few photos were submitted by families of the missing. There was no in-depth description of their last whereabouts, who they were with, nothing—just that they were black, white, or Latino, their age at the time of disappearance, and that they were still missing.

Chief Warren bellowed, "Lieutenant Rogers, come to the file room."

When he did, Chief Warren snatched the files from Officer Robinson and handed them to Lieutenant Rogers, who flipped through them in front of Mrs. Williams.

Shaking his head, Lieutenant Rogers looked up and said, "Mrs. Williams, I am so sorry about this. It's incredibly disturbing and alarming that no one has followed up on these reports. They are all marked 'RUNAWAY', and I am certain that is untrue. I am making a promise to you right now that a detective team will be assigned to this case file, and we will get to the bottom of it and find some answers for you and all the relatives of these children. Fresh eyes on these cases may bring a lot to the fold. Feel free to check in with Detective Jack Dillon as often as you feel necessary. Here is his card."

Lieutenant Rogers handed the card to Mrs. Williams, who was working hard at holding back her raging anger and tears as she said, "Thank you, Chief Warren and Lieutenant Rogers. I am at the end of my rope, and you just gave me and the other parents involved a tiny spark of hope."

JACK DILLON 1969

Special agent Detective Jack Dillon from the Chicago Police Department was ready to find out what had been happening with all the hushed cases in this city.

Detective Dillon was young, around thirty-four, clean-shaven, and had a close military cut of light, blonde, almost white hair that made his ears look a little too big. His angular jawline resembled a heroic cartoon character. His kind, commanding voice could be gentle or dominating and forceful. His experience outweighed his years.

His sky-blue eyes, speckled with yellow-green flecks, sparkled like a clear fall day. He was lean and muscular, barely under six feet tall, and intelligent, even brilliant, as his appraisals reported.

His eerie sixth sense about his cases led him down the right path almost one hundred percent of the time. He could be direct without sounding harsh and never missed a clue.

Most of all, he was fresh – fresh eyes and ears.

When he opened the file of all the missing kids over the past three years, he was outraged but not surprised that even white girls and teen boys, who always seemed to come first before women and girls of color in investigations, all had files in the drawer marked Missing Teens.

At that very moment, Jack Dillon decided to end this cycle. These missing kids were of the utmost importance, regardless of age, sex, or race.

Detective Dillon told the chief, "I need to appoint a female detective as a partner in this case since it is sensitive and involves so many young girls and women. I want to work with Liz Valentine."

Chief Warren radioed for Detective Liz Valentine to step into his office. Liz Valentine was a seasoned detective in assault, kidnapping, and trafficking cases involving young women, girls, and boys.

"Liz, I need you to assist Jack Dillon on some so-called missing runaway teen cases that have never been investigated. This is big. Please hand your current cases over to Detective Clancy so you can focus only on these files. I'll inform her that this is happening," explained Chief Warren.

Detective Valentine nodded, "This sounds extremely serious. I'll gladly work with Detective Dillon to solve these cases."

Liz Valentine was thirty-six years old and about 5 feet 4 inches tall. She had light auburn, almost copper-colored hair that shone like a new penny, pulled into a tight ponytail with a few wisps around her forehead and temples. Her skin was porcelain with a tint of pink and a lightly freckled, spreading around her nose and cheeks. Her eyes were clear and pure, as if shining from within. A translucent, not transparent, achromatic pale green with an azure blue ring around the rim, clear enough to allow light to pass through. Those eyes could stare at you without blinking, which made for severe interrogations.

Liz was a no-nonsense, thorough detective who could sleuth out and uncover things many other detectives could not. She questioned even the slightest clue. She had a commanding but gentle voice and wasn't afraid to get her hands dirty.

Detective Dillon nodded, "Thank you, Liz. We're going to stir things up just enough to get some answers."

They shook hands, and Chief Warren put one hand on each detective's shoulder as a gesture of trust.

Detectives Dillon and Valentine began by questioning everyone involved with the June Williams case, the latest missing girl.

Detective Dillon suggested to Valentine that they reverse engineer the case. "If we reverse engineer this case, it will most likely lead to solving more of the missing teen cases." Detective Valentine agreed.

They made a plan. "First, we speak to everyone involved in June Williams's disappearance."

Detective Valentine replied, "Yes, Mrs. Williams, the sisters, and Jimmy Barnes. I'll speak to Mrs. Williams, and we can split the sisters between us first. We should team up to speak with Jimmy."

"Sounds like a good plan," said Jack.

The detectives held files from the last thirty-six months. They discovered at least six missing teens. In one file, a farmhand found a girl's purple bicycle in a row of cornfields in April 1966. This discovery was the only thing charted. The missing girl was a young teen riding her bike after school.

After a notice was in the newspaper, including a photo of the bicycle, her parents recognized the bike and came into the station to report their daughter missing.

When interviewed, the notes in the chart stated that "Mr. and Mrs. Bernard Langdon reported their daughter as missing on April 22nd.

Her name is Julie. She is blonde, has brown eyes, is slightly under five feet tall, and is fourteen years old. Marked as a runaway."

Detective Dillon said, "Now, why would anyone assume that a runaway would leave their bicycle in a field?"

Detective Valentine replied, "Exactly, Jack. What else did you find in the next folder?"

"The next folder up is the Williams girl, June. This is a very current one. Time to closely review these folders precisely and make notes for similarities," said Jack.

SELENA May 9th 1969

When she got home from school, Iris told her parents that Selena was missing.

"Max and Selena's brother and all his friends are out looking for her. Everyone is saying that she ran away this morning. Mom, can we do something?" asked Iris.

Mrs. O'Brien said, "I'll call the station and find out how we can help search for her. And I'll call Dad to come home."

Moments later, Max burst through the door, "Mom, Selena is missing. The police told Mrs. Ortiz that the man working the ticket counter at the bus station said she was there. He wouldn't sell her a ticket since she is underage. He told the police that he had seen her sitting on the bench in front of the bus depot window, and when he looked again, she was gone. He got worried and called the police to report her as a possible runaway. Sebastian and I are searching for her anywhere we can think of."

"We're all going to help look, Max," said Mrs. O'Brien.

Iris called Lily to come over and help and to take notes on anything they saw or heard.

"Rose is looking for her sister, June, too." Lily said, "I think I might be able to get some information. Even the tiniest clues are overlooked sometimes. I'll be over in ten minutes. And I'll bring my camera."

"We went to the park and the library, checked the grocery stores, and asked her friends, but no one has seen her today. Oh, and we asked at the diner too. Stella said a girl was getting sandwiches and donuts at about 6 a.m. this morning. Based on her description, I think it was Selena. Mom, can we go to the police station?" Max asked urgently.

SELENA MID MORNING MAY 9TH 1969

"Hey, kid, are you OK? Do you need help or a ride?" a police officer said as he drove by Selena, who was sitting on the bus depot bench.

"Yes, can you take me to the train station downtown?" asked Selena. "The ticket I need is sold out here, and it will take forever to walk there," she said, telling a lie. But just a little one, she thought, since he didn't need to know.

"You want to go to Union Station?" the officer asked. "That's a big place for a kid to go by herself," the officer stated.

"I know, and I'll be fine. They should have the ticket I need since it's a bigger place," Selena argued. "I plan to call my mom to let her know I am there once I get to a payphone. And in case you're going to ask, I am eighteen." Selena tried to show no emotion.

"Well, I usually don't give rides like a taxi, but you look like you need help, and that's what cops do," said the officer.

The officer helped Selena get into the back seat of the police vehicle. She was hesitant but went anyway. "I should have asked to see his badge and ID," she thought. She had never been in a police car, and noticing no door handles or locks, an uneasy feeling crept into her body, making her swallow and clear her throat several times.

"So, where are you headed on the train?" asked the officer as he drove into traffic.

"I'm visiting my uncle in Texas," Selena said matter-of-factly, trying hard to show no weakness or distress.

"When is he expecting you?" said the officer.

"I'm supposed to call him before I board the train," she replied.

"I see," said the officer.

"What's your name?" asked Selena. "I'm Officer Davis," he replied.

Selena said, "I know Officer Robinson. He helped a bunch of us in the park last night."

"He's a fine Officer," confirmed Officer Davis. "A good guy."

Looking around at the street signs and buildings, Selena asked, "Is this the way to Union Station? I never went this way before."

"Yes, less traffic on this route," said Officer Davis, checking in his rearview mirror for her expression.

Selena became more apprehensive and uncomfortable and asked, "Could you pull over to that gas station so I can use the restroom?"

Officer Davis turned right to enter the gas station and pulled up to a pump.

"I'll fill up while we're here. You hurry on to the restroom and come right back. With this traffic, we still have about twenty minutes to the train station."

Selena went inside and watched Officer Davis wait for the service attendant to come outside and fuel his patrol car. Twenty more minutes?" she thought. That's a lot longer than how I've gone there with my mom. Why would he go this way?"

She asked the attendant at the counter for the restroom key. "Also, do you have a phone I could use?" she said, her eyes still fixed on Officer Davis in the parking lot.

"And please don't tell the officer I am on the phone." Selena made a mental note of the patrol car number and said softly aloud, "247."

"Sure, little lady, there's a payphone right next to the restroom door," said the attendant, handing her the key.

He headed outside to help Officer Davis. The attendant wondered what a young girl was doing with a police officer who looked so close to retirement age.

"Good afternoon, officer. Need a fill-up?" he asked. "Yes, I do," said Officer Davis. "And do you mind cleaning the windshield?"

"Will do," he said. The attendant intentionally took his time so the girl could use the phone inside. He had a feeling she needed privacy. He also thought it was strange that a police officer was filling up and asking for a clean windshield at a gas station. "Don't they do all that at the police station?" he said under his breath.

Selena searched for a back door by the restrooms so she could leave without being seen by Officer Davis.

There it was—a delivery door. She opened it enough to see a line of trees, a field, a few businesses, and houses. She quietly set the key on a supply box, pushed the door open just enough to squeeze out, and was sure to close it quickly and quietly.

She looked around and then ran like the boogeyman was chasing her because she felt like that was precisely what was happening.

She ran until she was down an embankment with a line of trees out of sight of the gas station. As she ran to a small row of houses, she knocked on the door of one of the few homes with a porch light on. An older woman opened the door, and Selena said breathlessly, "May I come in? Someone is chasing me."

"Oh my goodness, yes, child," the woman said.

"Do you have a telephone I could use to call my mother?" asked Selena.

"Yes, it's right in here," said the woman, leading Selena to the kitchen.

"Who is chasing you and why?" the woman asked.

"It's a police officer. I haven't done anything wrong. He said he was going to help me find the train station. But then he started asking me a bunch of personal questions, and I got scared," said Selena. "It didn't feel right."

"Well, you can stay here until your mother picks you up. And if any police come looking for you, I'll tell them I haven't seen you," the woman said.

"Oh, thank you so much," said Selena. "My name is Selena Ortiz."

The woman replied, "My name is Ruby Washington. Nice to meet you, Selena."

The phone rang three times on the other end. "Hello," said Mrs.

Ortiz.

"Mami, I need help. Can you come get me?" Mrs. Ortiz was relieved and happy to hear her daughter's voice on the phone, but concerned.

"I'm being chased by a police officer who picked me up at the bus station. I didn't do anything, Mami, I promise. But he was acting really strange," Selena said with a quiver in her voice.

"Yes, Selena. Where are you? Who are you with, and what is the address? Can you stay put until I can get there? Do not open the door for anyone," said Mrs. Ortiz, afraid her worst nightmare had come true.

Selena stayed with Ruby until her mother arrived. "Would you like some water or something to eat, dear?" asked Ruby.

"I would like some water, please. Thank you, Ms. Washington."

The doorbell rang. Ms. Washington opened it. Selena ran to her mother. "Mami! I am so sorry! This is Ms. Washington, and she is helping me. An Officer named Davis was giving me a ride to the train station, but he started going the wrong way, and I got scared."

Mrs. Ortiz held her daughter close and asked, "How did you get here?"

"I told him I needed to use the restroom. So he pulled over to that Sinclair station across from here. I went to the back, pretending to go to the restroom, and saw a delivery door. I went out that door and just ran!" Selena told her mother, trying her best not to cry.

"Oh, Mi Vida, that was a brave thing to do. But why did you run away in the first place? We talked about this last night. We've all been searching for you. Max, Sebastian, his friends, your friends. I'm so happy you are safe," said Mrs. Ortiz, holding her daughter's shoulders and looking into her eyes.

Mrs. Ortiz continued, "A man from the ticket counter at the bus station called the police to tell them he thought you were a runaway and in trouble. He gave a description, and we knew it was you. Did the police officer who was driving you know about this?"

"No, Mami, he didn't say anything," replied Selena.

"I think we need to report this," said Ruby, deeply concerned about Selena and her encounter. I will help you however I can."

Mrs. Ortiz called the police station from Ruby's home.

"Hello, this is Mrs. Lucia Ortiz. I found my daughter. She was at the bus station, just as the man there called in. But I found her on a different side of town. Is Officer Robinson available to speak to me?"

"Yes, he just returned from patrol," said the voice on the other end.

"Hello, Mrs. Oritz?" he asked. This is Officer Robinson. Do you have information on Selena?"

"Yes, Officer Robinson. We need to speak in private. Would you have time to meet with us at my home in an hour?" asked Mrs. Ortiz.

"Yes, I can do that," said Officer Robinson.

JUNE WILLIAMS May 10th, 1969

After scouring the neighborhood for hours, checking out the shops, restaurants, parks, schoolyards, and playgrounds, and asking if anyone had seen June, it was already almost 8 p.m., and it would be dark soon. The sisters went home to make a plan.

"Mom, she isn't anywhere! Should we call the police?" asked Maymie frantically.

"Yes, I will call, but it probably won't do much good," Mrs. Williams said as she wrung her hands and then pushed back some silver waves of hair that had come loose from her sapphire and goldenrod-colored scarf around her temples.

"They will only tell us that we have to wait forty-eight hours to report her missing. They'll tell me she just ran away and will come home when she's ready."

Everyone knew this was how things were, but that didn't stop Mrs. Williams from calling anyway. When she called, the officer she spoke to said those exact things to her.

"But Junie is not a runaway! She is an exceptional student who is happy, loves her family, and has lots of friends. And she's only twelve years old. We have searched for more than four hours all over the neighborhood, the school, the parks, the church, everywhere," implored Mrs. Williams.

After ten minutes of pleading her case on the phone, the officer finally agreed to send a car to patrol the area and would call her back if they found out anything. Mrs. Williams hung up the phone, and her head dropped hopelessly into her hands.

"I'm calling Iris and Lily to help search," Rose said emphatically.

"Did any of you girls tell Tony? He has some connections," Mrs. Williams said, organizing her thoughts.

"Mama, I went to the diner and asked if Mr. Tony could help us, and he said he would," Rose replied.

Iris and Lily arrived with Lily's girlfriend, Alice, to discover what was happening.

"Thank you for coming over so quickly," said Mrs. Williams.

Lily joined Iris, Max, and their friends and family, searching for June.

Lily carried a notebook, a pen, and a flashlight in her bag. She also brought her Swinger Polaroid camera and took pictures of anything she thought was suspicious or a possible clue, placing all the photos in an envelope in her shoulder bag.

Lily suggested that everyone split up into groups of two to cover the entire area. "I'll go with Rose. Iris and Denice can search together, and Alice and Maymie can pair up. That way, we can cover a lot of ground. Meet back here at 10 p.m."

"Sounds like a good plan," said Iris.

The friends split up, and all went in different directions.

Meeting back at the Williams home, each group of two discussed anything they found. "Tell us if you saw or heard anything," Rose said with hope and urgency.

"Not much luck here," said Maymie. We searched all over the school grounds and the playground and asked everyone there if they had seen Junie."

"No one saw or heard anything," Denice said, shaking her head. "The same thing happened with us as we walked the exact route she would have taken home from Tony's, and no one noticed a little girl who looked like Junie."

"We didn't find anything that she would have dropped, but we did notice tire tracks, like a car going too fast around the corner to home," said Rose. "We should tell the police about the tire tracks. Lily took some photos of the tracks."

Lily added, "At the diner, Stella said she heard screeching tires at some point, maybe around 2 p.m., but she looked out the window and didn't notice anything."

SUNDAY MORNING May 11th 1969

The next morning, the family could search more in-depth with the light of day. Rose walked along the sidewalks and into the street, following June's path home. Iris and Lily met up with Rose to look in all directions.

Rose reached the corner, crossed the street, and looked down toward the gutter and sewer grate.

"OH, NO," said Rose. Her heart pounded, and her stomach sank. "Those are Junie's!"

Before she could gather the colorful candy heart bracelet and a small bright yellow barrette in her hands, Lily called to her, "Rose, don't touch anything yet. I'm running over with my camera."

Rose's eyes burned, and tears rolled down her cheeks like the beginning of a summer rain. Lily took two Polaroids of the gutter and sewer grate where the items were.

"Look, Rose, look, Iris...see those tire tracks? A big car, truck, or something like that made those black marks on the street. It looks like someone screeched to a hard stop. I'll take a couple of pictures of those tracks, too," said Lily.

"Do you think it has anything to do with Junie?" asked Rose.

"I think it might," answered Lily, her tone serious.

"It looks like the bracelet and the barrette just fell off of Junie," Iris said, worried.

"Should I pick them up yet, Lily?" asked Rose.

"Yes, we'll put them in a separate envelope, then let's take them to the police with my photos," answered Lily.

Rose ran home and called, "MAMA, please come, please!"

Mrs. Williams ran to see what the commotion was.

"Rose, what is it? Did you find her?"

Rose couldn't speak. She held out her hand, which held the bracelet and barrette.

"NO, NO, NO," exclaimed Mrs. Williams. "I'm calling the police station immediately."

"I have some photos you can give to the police as well," Lily told Mrs. Williams. "It shows exactly where they were when Rose saw them. I also took two pictures of some black tire tracks that were curved. It looks like a big truck or something."

"I'm so grateful you took those pictures!" said Rose, placing her hand over her heart.

Mrs. Williams went directly to her phone and called the station.

"Hello, this is Mrs. Williams again. I spoke to an officer about my missing daughter yesterday."

"Yes, one moment, Mrs. Williams." The officer on duty said, "Mrs. Williams, it's Officer Robinson. How can I help you?"

"This is about my missing twelve-year-old daughter, June. We have searched almost nonstop since she did not come home on Saturday. My daughter, Rose, found some of her belongings in the gutter two doors from our home. Please help us."

"We'll send out a car to patrol the area. Please give me your address, and we will also call to inform you of anything we discover."

Mrs. Williams said urgently, "Thank you. I am so worried and frightened. We need to find her."

Two more days passed without a word from the police and no sight of June. Jimmy had not come home during this time either. Maymie was so distraught about June that she didn't notice his absence since he'd done this more than once during their relationship.

That morning, Mrs. Williams called the police station again.

"This is Mrs. Williams calling to see if there might be any news about June's disappearance. I was told a car would patrol the area where she disappeared. Why hasn't someone called, even to say you haven't found or heard anything? What about the bracelet and yellow barrette we found that belong to Junie?"

Mrs. Williams was strong and commanded the conversation as she wiped her tear-streaked cheeks. Her face burned like bare feet on summer-hot cement as she hung the phone back on the wall, but she would not back down.

"Girls, I am going to the police station to find some answers. Please stay here with the children."

When she arrived at the police station, Mrs. Williams was outwardly agitated as she approached the desk. "I need to speak to someone regarding my youngest daughter, who is missing," she stated as directly as possible, her eyes locked onto the officer at the desk. She had not seen this man before.

"Mrs. Williams, please follow me into this room." Mrs. Williams followed the officer into a small room with a table and three chairs, where another officer greeted her.

"Hello, Mrs. Williams. I am going to ask you some pertinent questions about your missing daughter. Please answer as honestly as possible while I fill out this report. What is her name and age? When was she last seen, where, and who was she with?"

The officer tilted his head shoulder to shoulder as if he had done this a thousand times and was only going through the motions as he wrote down her answers.

"June and her Uncle Jimmy went to Tony's Diner last Saturday. That's something they do frequently. She never came home, and we know Jimmy did not hurt her. He told us he had to go to work for a few days. June is twelve, and she is NOT a runaway.' Mrs. Williams was adamant.

"I have answered all the questions as clearly as I can. Now, how do we find my Junie?" Mrs. Williams asked as calmly as possible, feeling like her heart would crack into tiny pieces.

"My daughter, Rose, found these items in the gutter by the sewer drain two houses down from ours," said Mrs. Williams as she gently opened her hands to expose the envelopes with the bracelet, barrette, and Lily's photos. "I have some pictures our daughter and her friends took to show where these were and some tire tracks at the scene."

"Well, Mrs. Williams, she's probably a runaway. You wouldn't believe all the runaway reports we get this time of year."

There it was, he said it. Mrs. Williams was livid at this answer. Her voice became stern but tired.

"I have been over all of this with another officer, and I will repeat, she is not a runaway. Are you listening to me? Nothing is missing from her room. No one at school or from the neighborhood has seen her for almost three days. My daughter's partner, Jimmy, took Junie to get a milkshake at Tony's Diner, which they do regularly, but she never came home this time. And before you ask, he did not do anything to her. He loves her like a big brother, and they are very close. He takes very good care of her and protects her."

The officer nodded and said, "Mrs. Williams, I understand, but the protocol is that you must wait at least forty-eight hours. She'll come home when she's ready."

Mrs. Williams silently stood, then burst through the station door without saying a word, in a furor of rage and resentment that any mother of a missing child would display. She raised her fists to the sky, looking up, crying out, "Why, why can't someone help me? Where are you, Junie? I need to hear your voice! Call for me so I can find you, baby."

DILLON MAY 23ʳᵈ 1969

Over the next two weeks, Detective Dillon followed and staked out the silver truck with the blacked-out letters. He found numerous clues leading him to a rundown machine shed outside the city limits on a farm property behind rows of neighborhood businesses.

As Detective Dillon drove up the road, passing a cornfield to the farmhouse, he noticed no activity on the property. An old silver-gray armored truck, with the blacked-out letters on the side, was parked behind the house next to the shed, just as Jimmy described.

He walked around the truck, taking photographs of it. He walked around the shed, the area around the shed, and the perimeter of the farmhouse and field from all angles.

He heard no unusual noise or activity except for the scurry and high-pitched voicings of a few furry animals.

Dillon approached the truck and peered into the front window. It was messy with newspapers, food wrappers, a blanket, and some bottles and cans. He also noticed a plastic lunch pail between the two front seats.

"What's in that lunch pail?" he said suspiciously.

As he walked the perimeter of the one-story farmhouse, taking more photographs, he apprehensively knocked on the door. No one answered. Looking through the windows, he saw nothing strange at first sight. Detective Dillon had an eerie feeling about the silence and calm of this property.

He approached the large storage shed and listened. He heard something that sounded like a cat. The shed had one window with the blinds drawn and a steel door with a padlock.

At first glance, Detective Dillon didn't assume anything was strange since it was a storage building. But in his gut, he knew he had to pursue this hunch. He decided to return to CPD and put his team together to investigate.

JIMMY May 13th 1969

Jimmy returned after being gone for three days, which was not unusual for him. However, this time, he seemed abnormally jittery and nervous.

Maymie was frantic, asking, "Jimmy, where have you been, and what is wrong with you? Do you know where Junie is?"

He shook his head and said, "What do you mean, where's Junie? Isn't she here?"

"No, Jimmy, she isn't anywhere! Mama went to the police station for the second time. We've talked to them with no answers over these last three days. We searched all over town, but they are not helping us. They think she ran away. Where IS she?"

Jimmy put his hands on top of his head, rubbing them over his close-shaven head and then down his face, as his chin fell to his chest. "I'm sorry, I'm sorry. I don't know!"

"What are you talking about, Jimmy?" Maymie said angrily.

Jimmy now rubbed his hands together as if he were starting a fire.

"Maymie, I walked Junie down to Tony's for her favorite strawberry milkshake on Saturday. I didn't tell Junie I would be gone for a few days after we left the diner because she is always so sad when I'm gone for work, and she was so happy that afternoon. Since the diner is only a few blocks away, I told her she was old enough to walk home, and I would watch her until she got to the corner where home was, and I would see her later."

Maymie was livid as she yelled, "What? How could you do that?"

Jimmy was confused. "May, when we left the diner, I did not take my eyes off her. I watched her walk to the corner, where she turned to go home, and we waved to each other. Then, I waited a few more seconds so she could cross the street. Then, I turned around to go in the other direction. I checked for her one more time, and she was already around the corner and out of sight. So, I know she made it back home."

Maymie pushed Jimmy back hard with her hands on his chest, shouting, "She never got home, Jimmy! Where is she? What did you do with her?"

"I promise I am telling you the truth. I love Junie! I don't know what happened to her," he declared as he began to sweat. "I would never hurt her! She calls me her Superman."

Jimmy closed his eyes and pressed his fingers to his temples, thinking back three days.

"Wait, May, I remember something that caught my eye just as I started to walk back to the alley behind the diner. I saw a truck, you know, like an armored truck. It had some letters blacked out on the side, like a business name had been there, and no windows except for the windshield, the driver's window, and a passenger side window. It was speeding past me on the street. There was a police car right behind it, really close. I saw the driver of the truck, but didn't recognize him. The number on the police cruiser chasing the truck was 247. I remembered it because I had seen that car around here before, but I couldn't see the driver."

Jimmy continued, "I wondered why it was going so fast. I got scared that Junie might have been hit if she was crossing the street, but I didn't hear anything except the tires squealing around the corner. The people at the diner didn't notice anything, but I was outside, so I saw it."

When he said that to Maymie, a cold shiver shot through him like a blast of icy January wind.

"May, I'm sure I know this vehicle. I've seen the armored truck around before, but I don't know who was driving it or who it belongs to. When I saw it, I felt worried and aimed to run back to the house to check, but I stopped. In my gut, I didn't believe it."

Jimmy shook his head and said in a quiet, whispered tone, "Junie is OK. She made it home. She's OK. I can't say anything to anyone. I have to believe she got home."

Maymie broke into body-rocking sobs. "Tell the police, Jimmy! Tell them now!"

JIMMY AND TONY May 10th 1969

That Saturday afternoon, Jimmy had a promise to keep to someone. Someone he was nauseatingly afraid of disappointing, and he hoped the truck driver didn't see him. His stomach burned like a volcano, and he felt hot lava sliding straight up into his throat and mouth as he thought about where he was headed that afternoon and why he didn't walk June home.

Jimmy knew that Tony Rossini was not a man he wanted to tangle with for any reason, even though he showed his friends and customers another side of his personality, the good guy side. He has always taken good care of the Williams family since the day Eddie passed.

Tony was a broad giant of a man with a looming presence that towered over most men. He was around fifty and had thick muscles from his boxing gym and all the heavy lifting he did daily in the stock room. He was of white and Italian descent, and his thick black hair was slicked back like Elvis's, which was his nickname in certain circles. He had trimmed gray and black sideburns. His face was pockmarked, and he always had black and gray stubble. Tony had the darkest black eyes that shone like two black eight-balls, and he could stab sharply with a stare if angered. They could be terrifying and evil or almost kind, caring, and smiling with lines around those eyes like a beloved grandfather.

He had a hive of crude, ruthless men of all ages and descent in the background carrying out orders from him, whom he paid to execute his dirty work behind the scenes, because these men had nothing to lose. He was the head of one of the most well-known drug rings and money laundering operations in Chicago. He also paid for police protection due to his side activities. Jimmy knew this, but he had never seen a gray armored truck anywhere around Tony's or in the possession of the men he knew worked for Tony.

The diner was Tony's front for nefarious drug and money laundering activities ever since he bought it and moved in after the nightclub closed for good in 1962. Jimmy was only a young flunky recruited by one of Tony's boys. Jimmy's instructions were to keep his mouth shut, deliver the various packages, stay low, and return for his pay after the mission was finalized to Tony and the customer's satisfaction. Tony knew all the families in the surrounding neighborhoods and farther out from the Southside. Amid the gossip, he had a good reputation in the community as a happy, kind man who took good care of his customers and friends and called them family, especially Eddie's family.

Never before this one time had Jimmy ever let June go anywhere alone, especially where anyone from Tony's organization might see her alone, without supervision. Jimmy's only job was delivering drugs and paraphernalia. He was so frightened of this gang that he always did what he was told and never asked questions.

"I'm so stupid. How could I let Junie walk home alone? I watched her the entire time, and I can't believe this." Jimmy shouted under his breath as he pounded his fists into his forehead.

Maymie said, "Jimmy, you have to report this."

Jimmy anxiously said, "Report that I deliver drugs for Tony? That I let a little girl walk home alone?"

"Yes," said Maymie, "and you saw the truck and the police car and what time it was. Those cops know all about Tony's drug ring and how much money he makes. He pays them for protection. But YOU, you are just a little worker bee in a big hive, and you have to hold yourself accountable."

QUESTIONS AND ANSWERS

Any relative, friend, or neighbor of the missing children was called to the police station for an interview. Some of the cases were as old as 1960. As his calls were returned, interviews were set up, and the station became a hub of movement and gossip. Relatives from the oldest cases were set up to be questioned last, as the most current cases were more likely to lead to solving the entire caseload.

Family members and friends came in to be questioned one after another. The most consistent statement was, "The police told me I had to wait at least forty-eight hours to fill out a missing person's report."

Many tears fell, and every person who lost someone displayed anger, disillusionment, and rage. Detective Dillon told his partner, "Liz, I need you to work on this case with me. It's a highly sensitive matter and needs compassion and understanding."

Liz Valentine said, "I'm in, Jack. Let's get moving."

The two skilled detectives gently questioned everyone who may have seen, heard, or remembered something, including parents, neighbors, friends, teachers, and clergy, until they were all utterly exhausted. The detectives' stamina was superhuman when it came to missing children.

June's mother and sisters were questioned next. Mrs. Williams was so strong during questioning and told only the truth. "June is constantly in my care or the care of her sisters. She has never run away or even mentioned it. Junie is a happy girl with lots of friends. She makes good grades and loves school and life. She loves sports and has never been in trouble at school. She loves music and those strawberry milkshakes from Tony's Diner the most. She obeys the rules of our home and has never missed her curfew…until that day."

She continued, "Jimmy walked her to the diner for a strawberry milkshake. He loves Junie and enjoys taking her there once a week. But then we never saw her again that day, even after Jimmy came home three days later from work."

All three sisters gave identical testimonials. Detectives Dillon and Valentine had no suspicions that this wasn't the true story.

"Thank you, Mrs. Williams. You and your daughters have been extremely helpful." Detective Dillon told Mrs. Williams.

The detectives shook hands with the Williams family and sent them home for the time being.

The next person on the list to question was Jimmy Barnes, Maymie's partner. Jimmy entered the room, slumped into the chair, hands in his pockets, head down. The detectives glanced at each other.

"So, Jimmy Barnes, is that your name?" asked Dillon

Jimmy sat up straight and answered, "Yes, Sir."

Detective Dillon said, "What do you know about June Williams going missing on May 10th?"

Jimmy didn't speak for an agonizing amount of time. Jimmy eventually replied, "I don't know where she is. I only know that I walked her down to the diner for our Saturday strawberry milkshake."

"Go on," said Detective Valentine.

Jimmy continued, "Right after that, I had to be somewhere for my job. I told her she was old enough to walk the few blocks home and that I would watch her walk back home. She took off down the street, and everything was fine. I watched her turn the corner to our house. Then she waved to me to let me know she was OK before crossing the street. I figured she made it home just fine. Then I saw this gray armored truck. It looked like a bank truck, with the letters all blacked out."

Jimmy continued, "It was going fast in her direction, and a police car was tailing it. But I knew she had made it home. I saw her just a few steps away from our house. I felt so sick that I didn't walk her home the rest of the way. I was scared of being late because my boss would fire me--or worse. And I have to bring home money for our son and family."

Detective Valentine replied, "But, Jimmy, Maymie told us you were gone for three days. What kind of job do you have? Is that normal?"

Jimmy buried his head in his hands and started to weep quietly. "Yes, ma'am, that is normal. I can't say who I work for, or I may never make it home again."

Detective Dillon replied, "We have witnesses that saw you return to the diner after you let June walk home. The wait staff inside the diner saw you briefly. You went behind to the kitchen, then downstairs to the stock room, came back upstairs with a big manilla envelope, and then went out the back door of the diner. Is that correct?"

"Yes, Sir," said Jimmy. His voice was quivering and visibly shaking, and sweat rolled off him like a melting iceberg.

Detective Valentine handed him a small towel and a glass of water. She told him, "Breathe, Mr. Barnes."

Jimmy took a deep breath and said, "I saw that truck going in her direction. What if they hit her? What if they took her? I don't know why they would or where they would take her. I can't ask my boss, so what do I do? How can we find Junie? I'll do anything."

"Now that we know how she was probably taken, we're going to start pushing down hard to find her and the others," stated Detective Dillon, with a nod from Detective Valentine. "We need names."

"You're not in any trouble yet, Jimmy," added Dillon, but we want to collect your fingerprints." Jimmy nodded in approval.

Detective Valentine added, "We're fairly certain that your boss is running drugs. We are also concerned that you may be in harm's way. We'll keep you safe and let your family know."

Jimmy was held at the jail on a $500 bond until the detectives had more information. It was for his personal safety, and also so they could question him more when they needed to. After Jimmy confessed to letting June walk home alone even though he watched her almost all the way, keeping an eye on her as she walked, Detective Dillon said, "She was abducted by whoever was in that truck, Liz."

Detective Valentine replied, "And possibly the police car tailing the truck was part of it."

Mrs. Williams was called back in so the detectives could ask her if she had any indication that someone had kidnapped June, why, and who.

Mrs. Williams told them, "I have no idea. I know Jimmy didn't take her. Jimmy is a good man. He's you, and he gets himself backed into a corner once in a while and can't get out. I do know that he would never hurt her."

"Thank you for coming in again, Mrs. Williams. You've been extremely helpful, and we appreciate it. If you hear or see anything strange or relevant to this case, please call us here at the station, and we'll be glad to meet with you privately. We'll keep the barrette, candy heart bracelet, and photos for evidence," said Detective Valentine. "Be sure to thank the girl who took these pictures. It's a great help to us."

LILY AND IRIS May 14th

"I'm glad I got those photos to help the police," Lily told Iris. "I hope it helps lead to some information."

"I can't believe Junie is missing," said Iris. "And Selena, Max's girlfriend, is missing too," she continued. "What is going on in this city?"

The two friends looked at each other and had the same thoughts

"This is the beginning of our careers," said Lily. "We are helping the police find missing girls. And we will be part of the solution."

Lily and Iris felt like their contributions mattered to these investigations.

DILLION AND VALENTINE
FINDING ANSWERS

A tip line was set up, and news reports were broadcast to encourage anyone with information on missing children and teenagers in the city for the last three years or more to call the tip line.

Not many tips gave concrete information to pursue, but all tips were checked out. Most people calling in only wanted to know if there was a reward. After at least 100 false leads, an anonymous caller gave a tip:

"I know where some of those kids are." The caller left the name of Moose. "You can't call me back, but I will call you with more information tomorrow."

Dillon and Valentine attempted to trace the number and location of the call, but Moose hung up too fast. The next step was to interview Tony Rossini. The detectives went to Tony's Diner.

"Hello, is Tony here?" asked Dillon to the waitress at the counter. "Stella, is it?"

"Yes, it's Stella, and no, he is making a supply run to the food warehouse," said the thickset, bleached blonde waitress with a genuine smile and pink lip gloss.

"Would you like to have some of my fresh blueberry pie and wait for him to return?" she asked.

Detective Valentine noticed her name tag and asked, "Do you know how long that will be, Stella?"

"Oh, probably in about half an hour," she confirmed.

Valentine replied, "I think we'll come back in a bit. You don't have to tell him we were here, thanks!"

Detective Dillon winked at Stella, and she smiled at him with a girlish snicker, "OK, no problem." Looking at Detective Dillon, she smiled and winked back.

When they returned to the station, the detectives called Mrs. Williams. Detective Valentine said, "Mrs. Williams, can we send a car for you? We have a few more questions to ask."

"Yes, I'll be waiting," she replied.

When Mrs. Williams got to the station, the detectives took her back to the same room as before.

Detective Valentine began, "After Jimmy confessed to letting June walk home alone even though he watched her almost all the way, we need to let you know that Jimmy is in a holding cell for his protection."

Detective Valentine continued, "Mrs. Williams, do you have any indication that someone kidnapped June? Is there anything of hers missing, or would she have taken things with her if she wanted to run away? We don't believe she ran away, but we must check this out."

Mrs. Williams told them, "Nothing of hers is missing from home or her room. Her sisters and I triple-checked everything."

Detective Dillon said, "I understand. Thank you for coming in again, Mrs. Williams. You've been extremely helpful, and we appreciate it. If you hear or see anything strange or something that might be relevant to this case, please call us here at the station, and we'll be glad to meet with you privately anytime."

"Thank you for caring about my girl and all the missing children," said Mrs. Williams as she left the room. An officer took her back home.

As he pulled up to the Williams' home, the officer assisted Mrs. Williams to the front door and politely walked her into the living room.

The officer noticed a photo on the mantel in the front hallway. "Mrs. Williams, who are the men in this photo?"

Mrs. Williams replied, Oh, that's my late husband, Eddie, and his best friend, Raymond."

The officer said, "Thank you. Your husband's friend looks familiar."

Mrs. Williams replied, "Well, that's an old photograph, but it's my favorite of Eddie."

"It's a nice picture. Now, be sure to lock your doors and call us if you need anything."

Mrs. Williams nodded and thanked the officer, locking the door after he left. She turned around, putting her back against the door, and took a deep breath. "This is a nightmare," she said softly.

THE FARMHOUSE AUGUST 8TH 1969

Three months into the search, looking for young girls and women who had been missing for anywhere from one month to three years and longer, and questioning the friends and families of the missing, the farmhouse seemed to be empty, with no occupants every time the detectives attempted to enter during the past three months. The gray truck was consistently parked there, but no one was around. The shed was quiet, too.

After obtaining a search warrant, the detectives assembled a SWAT team to enter the suspicious abandoned structures and any vehicles on the property.

The farmhouse door opened quickly with one ram from the SWAT team. Entering the living room of the farmhouse, it looked in order.

The farmhouse was plain, with no actual color to the bland, old, worn furniture and gray walls. Only one picture with red, blue, and yellow blobs someone had painted hung on the wall above the beat-up dark green sofa. Dust was thick on the wood-panelled floor and furniture. Cobwebs were tangled in the higher corners of the walls and doorways.

Dillion told Valentine, "It's not very clean in here, but nothing seems to be in disarray."

As the team cautiously entered the home, weapons drawn, they cleared each room and let the detectives take the lead.

"I'll check the two bedrooms," said Valentine. Entering the bedrooms, Detective Valentine called to Dillon, "Hey, Jack, all the beds are only mattresses on the floor, bare of sheets or covers, with no bed frames. The mattresses are stained and filthy, but you can see imprints of a bed and frame if you look closely at the old carpet. So, who took the bed frames, and why? Check out the clothes on the floor and the mattresses."

"I'll have the team come in to photograph and collect all of this for evidence and forensic testing," said Dillon. "Check the closets, Liz. I bet we'll find something."

As Detective Valentine pushed the closet doors open, she said, "Jack, no way! Look at this! Different sizes and types of girls' and women's shoes, shorts, jeans, t-shirts, sweaters, purses, satchels, all in a sloppy pile. Dresses and other tops are on hangers, and high-heeled shoes are on the top shelf."

Valentine's eyes were brought to a girl-sized lime green T-shirt with bright yellow sunflowers. Old dried pink stains ran down the front of the shirt.

"Dillon, I'll bag this t-shirt and show it to Mrs. Williams. It might be June's. It matches the description of what she wore the day she disappeared."

"Let's gather up all of this for the lab, wear gloves for everything, and dust every surface for fingerprints," said Dillon as he directed the officers to the area.

"Jack, I'm going to the next bedroom to look in that closet," said Detective Valentine. As she opened the second bedroom closet, her flashlight clicked on brightly. "Oh my god, Jack, I can't believe what's in here!"

Detective Dillon quickly entered the room. "This is torture equipment," said Detective Dillon.

In the closet, they found a cattle prod, a branding iron, handcuffs, leather gloves, face masks, spiked leather neckpieces, a whip, duct tape, plastic bags, bottles of bleach and Pine Sol, and a wooden baseball bat leaning against the inside of the sliding closet doors.

The bathroom was a small room with a clawfoot tub and a toilet that had seen better days. The sink was stained with rust from the well water, and towels were hanging on two racks.

"Jack, I see a bar of soap in the bathroom, and the towels are fairly clean. When I ran the water, it ran rusty red for a few minutes and smelled like rotten eggs," said Valentine.

"Look at the walls, Liz, "said Dillon.

"Think that's blood spatter?" asked Liz.

Jack, taking multiple photos of every inch of the house, said, "I think it might be. We'll get photos and samples."

"What's this on the floor?" asked Liz, pointing and bending down on one knee to see better.

"Looks a lot like a child's Barbie doll with the legs missing," said Dillon. "Officers, get in here after you collect the clothing. Be sure to bag all this stuff to send to forensics and get them marked as evidence."

Detective Valentine added, "Let's head to the shed behind this house when you finish."

The team loaded up the evidence, and together, they went to the shed behind the farmhouse.

The metal machine shed had a steel door and a heavy, locked door handle. Dillon banged his fist on the door. "Hey, is anybody in there?" He called.

"I hear something," said Detective Valentine as she leaned in, pressing her ear against the steel door. "Did you hear that, Jack?"

"Yes," said Dillon, listening at the door.

Valentine motioned to the SWAT team, "Over here, team, break this door in, blast it, ram it, do whatever it takes to get it open."

The SWAT officers were able to break into the door by removing the screws that held the metal door handle. Reaching through the opening where the handle had been, they pulled the heavy door open.

Valentine noted and commented, "The only way to get into that shed is from the outside. There's no handle or lock on the inside of this door."

Time to call in DA Levine and the FBI," said Dillon.

Valentine ordered the SWAT team, "Team, dust for prints on every surface."

SELENA EARLY EVENING MAY 9th 1969

"Where's the girl who came in to use the restroom?" Officer Davis asked the gas station attendant. "Is she still in there?"

The attendant replied, "I gave her the key to the restroom but didn't see her come out yet since I was out at the pumps with you."

Officer Davis said, "I'm going back to check on her. Where is the restroom?"

"It's through that doorway on the left," said the attendant.

"Thanks," said Officer Davis. He went to the restroom door and knocked. "Hey kid, you in there?"

He banged his fist on the door, "HEY KID!" There was no answer, so he pushed the wooden door in with the back of his shoulder.

"She's not here. Do you have a back door?" Officer Davis asked the attendant angrily. He was breathing heavily and felt jittery. Losing this girl was going to cost him.

"Yes, sir, it's next to the supply cabinet behind you," said the attendant with some misgivings.

"I need to find her now before she gets in more trouble," said Officer Davis as he shoved the door open, only to see the row of houses, businesses, and a grassy field. He bolted out of the gas station. Officer Davis turned on his lights and sped out of the parking lot.

"Where are you, little girl? I'll find you." His demeanor changed dramatically. Now, Officer Davis was angry. Driving up and down the streets in this part of town, he knew she could be anywhere.

The gas station attendant called the police station. "Hello, this is Ted Whitaker, the attendant at the Sinclair gas station on State Street just outside the city. There was an older police officer with a teenage girl here a few minutes ago. She asked him to pull into the gas station so she could use the restroom. The girl looked scared and asked me for the restroom key and to use the pay phone. I think she ran out the back door."

Officer Robinson answered the phone and asked, "Do you know the officer's name and the girl?"

"His name is Officer Davis. I don't know her name, but she is about 15 or 16, pretty, and looks Spanish or Mexican. She was nice, but I could tell she was scared. She may have run to one of the businesses or houses behind my station."

The officer asked, "Do you remember if she was carrying anything or what she was wearing, or can you describe anything else about her?"

"I noticed she had a dark high school jacket. I think it was navy blue. She had a dark scarf tied under her chin and white tennis shoes," said Ted. "Oh, and she was carrying a leather shoulder bag."

"Thank you, Mr. Whitaker, this is very helpful."

"Anytime," said Ted, "I am worried about her safety."

"So are we," said the officer.

SELENA 7 p.m. MAY 9th 1969

Officer Robinson arrived at the Ortiz home later that evening.

"Thank you for coming, Officer Robinson," said Mrs. Ortiz.

"Can you tell me what's happening with Selena, her reasons for running away, and how she ended up at Ruby Washington's home?" asked Officer Robinson.

"Selena, please tell Officer Robinson what happened," said Mrs. Ortiz. Sitting in a chair across the living room from Officer Robinson, Selena sat up straight, hands folded in her lap, and nodded.

"Officer Robinson, first, I want to apologize for this situation. When you saw us in the park the other night, I was talking to Max about running away." Selena said, looking up at her mom, ashamed. "I was so angry and sick of Sebastian and his gang friends telling me what to do, who I could see, and controlling my life. It sounds pretty dumb now, but I felt like it was my only option." Selena said as she bowed her head.

"Go on, Selena," said Officer Robinson.

"Well, Max and I started talking, and then Sebastian and his gang came up and pulled me away from Max. I didn't want them to see me cry, so I just got mad. Sebastian told Max to stay away from me, and then I thought they were going to start fighting. I was so nervous. But then you pulled up." Selena tried to smile at the officer.

"Did all of you kids go home like I told you to do?" asked Officer Robinson.

"Yes," said Selena. "Then I just went to my room and pretended to get ready for bed. But I just wanted to leave. I was planning to jump out of my window, but I decided to lie down for a few minutes and rest. By the time I woke up, it was 5:30 in the morning, and I knew my mom would be coming to tell me to get ready for school."

Officer Robinson asked, "What do you do then?"

Selena answered, "I put on some dark clothes and a scarf, threw my bag out of the window, and jumped out. I ran to Tony's in town to get some food for later. I was scared because I think Stella saw who I was." Selena started to feel her eyes burning as a tear rolled down her cheek.

"Then I went to the bus station to get a ticket to my Uncle's place in Texas. He didn't know I was coming."

"Go on," said Officer Robinson, making notes.

"The man at the counter wouldn't sell me a ticket and told me to get out of the line since I'm not eighteen. I told him I was, but didn't have any ID." Selena replied, bowing her head.

"Did you leave at that time?" asked the officer.

"Yes, I just sat on the bench outside the bus station, making a new plan," said Selena.

"What happened next?" asked the officer.

Selena nervously replied, "A police car drove past and stopped to ask me if I needed help. I didn't know the officer but told him I needed to get to the train station. He said he wasn't supposed to give rides like a taxi, but he let me in the car anyway, saying he would help me.

I asked him his name, and he said he was Officer Davis. He was an older man. I noticed we were not going in the right direction from the train station, and it scared me. So I asked him to pull over so I could use the restroom at the Sinclair."

"Did he pull over?" asked Officer Robinson.

"Yes, he pulled over and said I could go in, but to hurry while the attendant filled up his car. I got the restroom key, but I didn't go in. I looked for a back door and found a delivery door. I opened it to look around, then I went outside, closed it, and ran as fast as I could to get out of sight. I didn't want him to see me. Then I saw a few houses. Ms. Washington's porch light was on, so I knocked, and she let me in. That's when I called my mom." Selena's voice grew nervously louder as she explained.

"Selena, I want you to know that the gas station attendant called the station to report this. You were right to run to Ms. Washington's house, but this was all very dangerous," Officer Robinson explained.

"I know," said Selena, putting her hands to her forehead, dropping her chin. "And I am so sorry that I caused these problems for everyone."

"You may have helped us solve a few problems unexpectedly, Selena. There have been some child abductions recently. You might have been one, but you got away. Please stay close to home and your mother." Said the officer.

"Oh, Officer Robinson, I will, I will! I promise to pay attention to my mom and be sure she knows where I am at all times," said Selena.

Officer Robinson asked Selena, "Do you remember a number on the police car?"

"Yes, I do," said Selena, excited that she remembered. "The car number was 247."

"Great memory, that helps a lot, Selena," said Officer Robinson.

"Mrs. Ortiz, thank you for calling me and getting Selena home safely. I'll look into this when I return to the station," said Officer Robinson.

Mrs. Ortiz thanked him as she walked him to the door. After Officer Robinson left, she closed and locked it.

"Selena, I want you to feel certain you can always come to me with any problems." Mrs. Ortiz continued, "I know Sebastian can be overbearing sometimes, just like your father. I also know he loves you and wants to keep you safe. We'll figure it all out with him. I love you both and want us to have a happy home."

Selena hugged her mom and felt her mother's warmth pass into her. It was the calmest she had felt in a long time. With her mother's arms around her and her head on her mother's chest, she felt all of the tension and anxiety melt away. "I love you, Mami." Said Selena.

"I love you too, Mi Vida." Said Mrs. Ortiz.

OFFICER DAVIS FRIDAY NIGHT, MAY 9th 1969

"Has anyone seen or heard from Patrol Officer Davis this evening?" asked Lieutenant Rogers.

"No one has seen him after his morning shift," answered the officers in the room.

"Where is his cruiser?" asked Lieutenant Rogers.

"It looks like it's checked out but never checked back in for today," answered the desk officer. "I'll speak to Captain Burrows," Rogers confirmed.

Just then, Officer Robinson walked into the office. "Lieutenant Rogers, may I speak to you privately?" asked Officer Robinson.

"Yes, step into my office," replied the Lieutenant.

They sat on chairs on opposite sides of the desk. "I think we have a problem," said Officer Robinson.

"Fill me in," said the Lieutenant.

"Officer Davis may be dealing in some things that are not exactly legal," said Officer Robinson. "Today, he picked up a teenage girl at the bus station and offered to take her to the train station. She told him she needed help to get there. He then drove in a different direction. She was aware of going the wrong direction and asked him to stop at a gas station to use the restroom."

"And you're sure it was Davis?" asked the Lieutenant.

"Yes, I spoke to the girl and her mother just now. Davis pulled into the gas station to let the girl use the restroom. He then continued to have the attendant fill up his patrol car while he waited for her."

"That is very odd," said Lieutenant Rogers. "We don't fill up at gas stations. We use the municipal fueling station."

"Right. The girl went to the back, but instead of using the restroom, she sneaked out the delivery door and ran to some houses behind the station." Officer Robinson said.

He continued, "She knocked on the door of Ruby Washington's home. Ms. Washington let her in to use the phone and call her mother, who came to pick her up. Her mother then called me to take a statement."

"This girl asked the officer for his name. The name he gave was Officer Davis," Robinson clarified.

"Good for her to ask his name. You mean to tell me Ray Davis did this? Why, he's close to retirement." Lieutenant Rogers said.

"Yes, I know, and I'm not sure what's going on with him," said Officer Robinson.

"Thank you for this information, Robinson. This will be looked into immediately."

"I also have some questions about Captain Burrows," added Officer Robinson. "May I talk with you later?"

At that exact moment, the officer who had driven Mrs. Williams home after her visit with the detectives walked in.

"Hey, Luis," called Lieutenant Rogers. "Come in here, please."

"What's up, Lieutenant?" asked Officer Luis Perez. "How well do you know Officer Ray Davis?"

"Not too well, why do you ask?" said Officer Perez. "But now that I think of it, when I escorted Mrs. Williams into her home just now, I saw a picture on her mantel of her late husband and a man she called Ray, who was her late husband's best friend. He looked a lot like Officer Davis, but younger."

Lieutenant Rogers contacted Detectives Dillon and Valentine. "Jack and Liz, we want to ask Jimmy Barnes a few more questions. Can you come to the station?"

"Yep," said Dillon. "We'll be there shortly. Meet in room two."

"Come on in, Jimmy. We have a few more questions for you. Hopefully, they will jog your memory," said Dillon.

Meeting with the detectives in Room Two, a smaller room than the other interrogation rooms, made Jimmy feel like he was being squeezed, and he undeniably felt it.

"Jimmy, do you recall a photo on the mantel at your home? It's a picture of Eddie Williams and another man?" asked Dillon.

"Yes, I know there's a picture on the mantel, but let me think," said Jimmy.

"Take your time," said Dillon.

"It's an old photo of Eddie, Mr. Williams, and another man. WAIT, now I know where I've seen the other man."

"Go on, Jimmy," said Detective Valentine.

"That's the man I sometimes see in the back booth at Tony's Diner when I go there. I don't know his name, but I see him there every weekend." Jimmy told the detectives.

"I saw him the day Junie and I went there, and I was racking my brain to think of where I had seen him before. And it's not just because he's always there. It's that picture. He is the man in the picture," said Jimmy.

Jimmy continued, "He always seems to have his eyes on Rose Williams when she works there. Rose waits tables and works the counter. And he watches other teenagers as they come in on Saturdays. I should have paid closer attention to him and how he stares."

"Does the name Raymond Davis mean anything to you, Jimmy?" asked Dillon.

"I think I've heard the name before. Mama Williams has mentioned that he was Eddie's best friend. But I don't know anything about him," Jimmy told the detectives.

"Thanks so much, Jimmy," said Detective Dillon. "This is a great help in possibly solving this case and probably more like it."

"Jimmy, I want to keep you here for a while longer while we investigate. You can go as soon as we know it's safe," said Valentine.

THE SHED AUGUST 8th 1969

As the SWAT team pulled the heavy shed door open, Detective Valentine saw five young girls sitting on the dirt and concrete floor. Some had collapsed, and some had opened their eyes slightly.

Weak, heads hanging, filthy, and too emaciated to be scared anymore, they had been constantly drugged, violated sexually, and physically abused. They were shackled, one arm to iron pipes, one leg to each other, and mistreated to the point of death for one of the five girls in the machine shed. The violence that happened here felt inconceivable.

They had all been exposed to the elements—extreme heat and bone-chilling cold. Mice and other wildlife entered the building through the walls and under the floor. Some had open wounds where mice and other rodents had bitten and scratched their legs and arms.

There was a tray with old, unidentifiable food that the mice and rats had been eating, three empty jugs of water, and two blue plastic buckets full of excrement set in a corner for the girls, if they could even make it to the buckets.

The odor of urine, waste, infection, and death was paralyzing, causing Detective Dillon and the officers to clutch their chests, coughing, and some of them breaking down into body-shaking sobs. They were shattered.

"These children are being sold. They don't even know what day it is or who is doing this. They are being drugged, probably overdosed, and sold as slaves to the highest bidders," said Valentine emotionally. She continued, "I'm radioing for ambulances and help to get them to the hospital."

"Evans and Carson, you two search every inch of this slave shed. Photograph everything you find, everything you see. Wear your gloves, and do not touch anything without them on. Use the evidence bags for all of it," ordered Dillon. "We have to keep all the evidence until forensics can test it. Dust every surface for fingerprints."

Then Dillon walked over to the only window in the building and pulled the cord to open the worn, torn, filthy, and stained shade and blinds, allowing some light into the place. The window appeared to have been painted over, then the paint scratched off.

He noticed a metal desk near the back of the room with a drawer in the middle and three stacked drawers on the right side. None of the desk drawers was locked.

As he pulled them open one by one, Dillon exclaimed, "Oh man, Valentine, look at this."

The drawers were full of needles, some used, some new, vials of some liquid, bottles of pills, and dirty hospital gloves and gowns. One drawer had used lingerie, hair brushes, makeup, and costume jewelry. Another drawer held bath soaps, shampoo, and a few 'sort of' clean bath towels.

"These girls are children. How can this happen?" Valentine was infuriated.

"We're going to get this figured out, but first, we'll take care of these girls," said Dillon.

The young girls, two black, two white, and one Latino, had no identification and were clad only in underwear, torn lingerie, tank tops, and no shoes. One of the young girls was pregnant. One was deceased.

When the officers asked each girl if they knew who they were and where they were, one of them said quietly, in a shaky, breathy whisper, "I-I know who I am. But I don't know where this is."

Another said, in a tiny, weak voice, "Who are you? Are you taking us somewhere again? I don't want to see that man."

The officers reassured them that they were finally safe and that they were the police, taking them all to the hospital. The EMTs wrapped the girls in blankets, even though it was sunny and extremely warm that day.

One girl was not in the same area as the other five. She peeked out from behind a wall divider. "Hello? Is it OK to come out?" said a little voice.

Detective Valentine said, "Yes, come on out here and tell us who you are and what has happened to you. We're here to help."

"My name is June Williams. I remember a little of what happened."

"Hello, June Williams," said Valentine in a soft voice. "I'm Detective Liz Valentine. Can you tell me anything you remember about being here or how long you've been here?"

June replied, "I'm not sure how I got here, but I remember walking home, and someone grabbed me. Then everything went dark.

I didn't know where I was until I woke up. Then they brought me here and told me to change my clothes. They gave me some shiny adult-type nighty thing that was really short."

Detective Valentine asked, "Did you do what they told you?"

"Yes, ma'am, I did," said June.

"Where are the clothes you had on, and what happened when you changed your clothes, June?" asked Valentine.

"I think my clothes are in a closet somewhere. I was very nervous. But the woman said she wanted to take some pictures of me like a model," said June, placing one hand on her hip.

"Is that what she did?" asked Valentine.

"Yes, she took lots of pictures of me and kept saying, 'This one is special, very beautiful, very young, and will bring in lots of business,' but I didn't know what she meant," said June, confused.

"Let's get you checked out at the hospital and then home as soon as we can," said Valentine, crouching down to June's height, but being very careful not to touch or scare her. "You can tell me the whole story once you are safe and settled into a room at the medical center. How old are you, June?"

"Umm, what day is it? Did I miss my thirteenth birthday? I'm twelve if it's before October," said June.

"Yes, it's August, and I'm happy to say that you will turn thirteen with your family in October," said Valentine, helping the EMTs get June into the ambulance.

"Oh, thank you. I've been super scared this whole time. And the other girls, are they going to be all right? They've been here a long time. And I don't like the pills they give us. They make me so sleepy," said June with disdain.

The detectives and their assistant officers wasted no time scouring the rest of the shed for evidence. They dusted for fingerprints and collected anything belonging to the girls and their captors. A large metal box was found on a splintered wooden shelf against one of the walls. It contained several Polaroids stashed in a square Manila envelope. Also inside the box were seven partially destroyed IDs and fake identification papers.

Only four of the IDs helped to identify the girls in the shed. There was no ID for the pregnant girl. When questioned, this girl had no idea where or who she was and had no recollection of what had happened to her.

A school identification card with the name Julie Langdon resembled the deceased girl.

The photographs of each girl seemed to have been taken just after they were abducted. The officers found two torched driver's licenses, a pair of tortoise-rimmed eyeglasses from one of the girls, a necklace of multicolored plastic beads that a child would wear, a solid gold bracelet, blue earrings that looked like they may have been birthstone earrings, and a man's pinky ring with a red stone that Detective Valentine guessed to be a garnet or a ruby, with the initials EW inscribed along the inside the gold band with a symbol that might have been a Roman Numeral.

Other items were seized, such as liquid vials, liquor bottles, more needles, and a small, car-sized first aid kit that would fit in a glove compartment. The first aid kit was empty except for one box of old Band-Aids, iodine, gauze, and medical tape.

More silver duct tape was found on one of the shelves under a few plastic bags. The plastic lunch box Dillon had seen in the truck earlier was also there. The plastic box contained an alarm clock and a notebook containing a list of names, including alias names for the girls, such as Penny, Sugar, Sweetie Pie, Candy, Cherry, Coco, Blondie, Cinnamon, and others. Inside the notebook were more than twenty bogus names of young girls.

"Where are the rest of those girls? Are they alive?" Detective Dillon asked, looking at Detective Valentine for some kind of answers.

Valentine shook her head in sadness and disgust. "I don't know, but we WILL get to the bottom of this."

Also found inside the box was a small black address book with the names, phone numbers, and addresses of what appeared to be at least thirty male clients. Some of the alias names were written next to each client's information.

Detective Dillon, trying to decipher this puzzle, thinking aloud, "Were they sold? Did they escape and run away? We'll begin this search with the address book and see how far we can get."

THE HOSPITAL, AUGUST 8th 1969

The deceased girl was taken to the medical examiner for forensics and an autopsy as the detectives and police worked furiously to find out who each victim was and contact their families.

"Look through the files and find all the names of the missing girls between the ages of eleven and sixteen," said Dillon to an officer at the station using a hospital phone.

All the girls were identified through questioning, except for the deceased girl. She was young, blonde, and so emaciated that she appeared very small and possibly younger than her actual age. It was hard to tell much more about her.

"She looks no older than twelve or thirteen years old," said Valentine with a noticeable shudder in her voice. "She did nothing to deserve this. No child deserves this."

As each family was contacted, the parents met at the hospital, except for the family of the deceased girl, whose parents met with the medical examiner to identify the body.

An autopsy showed that her body was saturated with different types of drugs. She had numerous needle marks on her arms, legs, and even on the top of her feet. She was severely malnourished, dehydrated, beaten, and had been violated multiple times. She had been suffocated and bludgeoned. It appeared she had been held captive longer than the other girls. The medical examiner documented her death as a homicide from blunt force trauma and suffocation.

Pulling old records of a missing girl who left her purple bicycle in a cornfield, the officer helping Dillon and Valentine was able to locate the parents of Julie Langdon. Detective Valentine called Julie's mother to meet her at the hospital.

"Oh my god, my husband and I will be there in ten minutes," said Mrs. Langdon.

When the Langdons met with Detectives Dillon and Valentine, they introduced them to the medical examiner.

As the Medical Examiner pulled the sheet away so they could see Julie's face, the parents identified her as their missing daughter.

Mrs. Langdon grasped her husband's arm and lost her balance. "This is my Julie," she said. Her voice was very weak and hoarse. "She was only twelve when she disappeared in 1966. Her fifteenth birthday was just last week." Mrs. Langdon began to sob.

"We've identified Julie from her dental records and need your identification for her death certificate," said the M.E. in a firm but gentle voice. "I'm so very sorry about what has happened, Mr. and Mrs. Langdon."

"We'll explain everything to you once we have all the facts," said Detective Dillon. "We're so sorry for your loss."

"Thank you for bringing our girl back home. We need closure," said Mr. Langdon. "Now we can let our daughter finally rest in peace."

"We'll be in touch as soon as we know more. Please accept our condolences," Detective Valentine said as she gently touched Mrs. Langdon's arm.

Mrs. Langdon reached out to Detective Valentine and wrapped her arms around her, holding back her sobs. "Thank you; she's home now," Mrs. Langdon said as she released her hug and touched her hands together in prayer.

THE HOSPITAL AUGUST 8th 1969

When asked, June knew what had happened. She had been listening and paying attention whenever possible while captive.

"I saw what happened to her. They called her Candy, but I know that wasn't her real name because she never responded to it until they called that name two or three times."

June continued, "She would say, 'That's not my name. Julie is my name.' Then she would tell them she wanted to go home." June's voice got louder and angry.

A female officer was put outside June's hospital room for protection, while another was inside the room. The nurse held June's hand and tried to ask her easy questions, but nothing about this was easy.

The female officer, Officer Chase, in June's hospital room, asked if she could tell her how the girl died.

June laid her head on the arm of the nurse, looked down, and said, "Well, I saw her get hit pretty hard in the back of her head and her stomach with something that looked like a short baseball bat because she wouldn't stop screaming and crying. I was so scared it would happen to me, so I stayed as quiet as I could, but I wanted to cry."

"You were so brave, June. Can you tell us more?" asked Officer Chase.

June looked up at Officer Chase, still holding her nurse's arm, and said, "Then, after she had been quiet for a while, she started crying and screaming again. I thought she was seriously hurt because she wouldn't stop. So they stuffed a sock or something in her mouth and put a plastic bag over her head. Except they forgot to remove it when she stopped screaming and squirming." June shivered.

After speaking, it brought back the terrible memories, and June began to weep in waves.

"You're safe now, June," said the nurse as she gently took her tiny hands and warmly caressed them with both of her hands.

Kindly laying her hand softly on June's shoulder, Officer Chase said, "Thank you for being so strong, June. Your mother is on the way here right now. She will be so happy to see you."

"Just push this button on the side of the bed if you need me for anything," said the nurse as she left June alone with Officer Chase, who stayed in the room with June.

In the other bed was the pregnant girl.

"What will happen to her?" June asked the officer.

"Oh, June, I'm not sure yet. They will check her fully to see if she and her baby are all right and then get her as healthy as possible."

June turned to look at her hospital roommate, who was still sleeping. "I hope she wakes up and is OK," she said with her hands crossed on her chest, and more sobs.

When Mrs. Williams was contacted, she immediately went to the hospital. When she got to June's hospital room, she could see her little daughter sleeping.

She let out a wail full of relief and sorrow so big that it resonated throughout the building. The wailing turned into moaning and sobbing.

"My baby, my beautiful Junie. Why did this happen…why? Oh, Junie, you've always been such a smart girl and a sweet, kind, and caring child. Why would someone try to take you from me?"

Mrs. Williams collapsed to the floor. The staff brought a wheelchair to help Mrs. Williams since she could no longer stand on her unsteady legs. She shook uncontrollably with her head in her hands, weeping and shaking her head.

As soon as she was calmer, the nurse asked if she was ready to go in.

"Yes, yes, please. I need to touch my daughter and make sure she is all right. I need her to see me, and I need to look in her eyes," said Mrs. Williams.

They wheeled her into June's room and to her bedside.

Mrs. Williams touched June's little face. She saw a reddish, blue bruise on her left cheekbone under her soft amber eyes.

"Mama," said June. "Mama, I knew you would find me." Her eyes were fixed on her mother as tears and sobs shook her little body. "Mama, I tried so hard to be brave."

"What happened, Junie?" Mrs. Williams asked, holding back her anxiety and tears.

"Yes, June, can you explain what happened to you?" Officer Chase asked.

"I don't remember a lot. But I know I was walking on the sidewalk in front of our house, and a man jumped out of a truck and grabbed me so fast I heard tires squealing!"

"Then what happened, baby girl?" asked Mrs. Williams as the officer wrote down everything June said.

"All I know is that he covered my mouth with his big smelly hand and gave me a shot in my neck, not in my arm like at the doctor."

"Go on, sweetheart," said Mrs. Williams.

"Then I remember just waking up in this horrible, ugly, dirty room. Oh, Mama, it smelled terrible. The floor was hard and had a big layer of dirt. There were mice and rats!"

"The man who grabbed me told me to sit on the floor, then showed me to a woman named DeeDee or something like that. She wanted to take pictures of me. I asked her why, and she told me I was so pretty that she wanted me to model for them. She told me I was special, not like the other girls, and that I could go far and make a lot of money."

The officer told June, "June, you are so courageous. What happened after she took your pictures?"

June thought momentarily, then said, "They wanted me to change my clothes and take more pictures like models do for photo shoots."

"What did they want you to wear?" asked Officer Chase, taking notes.

"They gave me this old shiny nightie with a couple of holes in the back of it and told me I had to leave my shoes off," said June. "It would have been kind of pretty if it didn't have the holes. I don't think they knew my name because they called me Coco. I had to get used to that name so I wouldn't get in trouble like Julie did if I didn't answer when they said that name."

June continued looking at her mother, "Mama, they took my favorite T-shirt with the yellow sunflowers. That made me sad."

June continued taking deep breaths. "But I always did what I was told so I wouldn't get in trouble, except when they kept giving me those pills. Sometimes, I tried to keep the pill under my tongue and spit it out when no one was looking."

"That was good, June," said Officer Chase. "Were you able to do that?"

"Only one time," said June. "They always watched me after that one time."

"Is there anything else you can tell us?" asked Officer Chase.

June said, "Yes, I saw DeeDee or Delores, or whatever her name was, giving pills to the other girls. Then, when the pictures were done, they gave me one of the pills. I didn't want it, so the man hit me. I tried my hardest not to cry, but it hurt. Then I took the pill. It made me sleepy."

"Did that happen more than once?" Officer Chase asked.

"Yes, he hit me again a couple of days ago for not taking the pill," said June. "DeeDee told him not to mess up my pretty face."

"Then, a man wearing a suit and tie came in and looked at all of us. He pointed at Cinnamon and handed that woman some money."

"What happened with Cinnamon after that?" asked the officer.

Mrs. Williams squeezed Junie's little hand and pushed the hair back from Junie's smooth forehead. "Go ahead, Junie, tell Officer Chase what happened next if you can."

June said, "OK, Mama. The next thing I saw was another man, maybe the one who hit me, take a key from DeeDee and unlock Cinnamon so she could stand up. But DeeDee had to help her get up. The man with the money took her outside. I don't know what happened after that."

"June," said Officer Chase, "I have two more questions for you, and that's all for tonight."

"OK," June said. She was completely exhausted.

"Do you remember seeing a farmhouse on the other side of the shed you and the other girls were in?"

"No," said June, "I heard some people going in and out of the shed, but I didn't see the house or anything else."

"Good job," said Officer Chase. "June, can you describe the man who unlocked Cinnamon's chains?"

"I tried not to stare so no one would notice, but I looked up, and I could tell he was older, black, and he always did what DeeDee, um, or Delores told him to do," said June. "Mama, he looked a little like Daddy's friend in the picture at home. Was it him?"

"Oh, baby girl," said Mrs. Williams, holding June's hand tightly, "You have sure been through a lot."

"Mama, when can I come home?" asked June.

The nurse said, "June, we'd like you to stay tonight and tomorrow. Then, the doctor will check you to see if you are well enough to go home. How does that sound? You can also get some ice cream and eat whatever you want from the cafeteria. Just tell me what you would like!"

"That sounds good to me!" June exclaimed. "Do you have strawberry ice cream? And could I have a hot dog?"

"We sure do, and yes, you can have a hot dog," said the nurse, smiling kindly.

June asked, "What about Cherry and her baby?"

The nurse said, "We are going to take extra good care of them, so don't you worry. And if she wakes up and can talk, you can say hello to her."

"Thank you. I'd like that," June replied, putting her hands on her face, then reaching out for her mother.

SELENA May 12th 1969

After the incident with Officer Davis, Selena felt much closer to her family. By Monday, she was ready to go to school and try harder to make herself and her mother proud.

She got up early, got dressed, finished her homework, and went to the kitchen for breakfast. Her mother made her a special meal of scrambled eggs and churros with extra cinnamon and sugar.

"Oh, thank you, Mami! This is delicious, and I am so hungry," said Selena.

"You're welcome, little daughter," said Mrs. Ortiz. "You will have energy all morning. Here is a glass of milk to top it off. Better than a couple of peanut butter sandwiches and a donut, right?" Selena and her mom laughed cautiously; everything felt much lighter than yesterday.

"Is Sebastian here?" asked Selena.

"No, he is off to look for a job! Can you believe it?" said Mrs. Ortiz. "I'm pretty sure he was so frightened that you were hurt or something that he has decided to work harder to make this family better."

"I'm so happy, Mami! I will give him a big hug tonight!"

"Have a good day at school, and if you see or hear anything that feels wrong, be sure to tell your teacher to call me," said Mrs. Ortiz.

"OK, Mami, I will! I love you, and I'll see you this afternoon."

Then Selena grabbed another churro and her school bag and

headed out the door to catch the bus.

As Selena walked down her street to the school bus stop, she noticed a car following her. Her body froze. It was not Officer Davis but another officer in a different-numbered patrol car. Why was he following her and watching her so closely? Selena wondered if she really was in some kind of trouble.

Not knowing whether to run or blend in with the other kids at the bus stop, she decided to walk faster and pretend she didn't see him.

"Mami said to tell the teacher if something strange happened today," said Selena softly. "I feel so uncomfortable again. What is going on?"

When she got to school, Selena took her teacher aside to ask her to call her mother. "Are you feeling all right, Selena?" the teacher asked.

Selena replied, "Yes, but something weird happened at the bus stop."

"All right, you go to class, and I'll ask the secretary to call your mother. Then I'll be right in to start class."

"Oh, thank you," said Selena.

Selena was pulled out of her class an hour later to meet with her mother and the school principal.

"What happened, Selena? asked Mrs. Ortiz. "Mrs. Lipowski said something strange happened at the bus stop this morning."

"Yes, Mami," Selena continued, "Another police car was

watching and following me. It was a different officer driving and a different car number."

Mrs. Ortiz turned to Mrs. Lipowski and asked, "Mrs. Lipowski, is there anything we can do to ensure Selena's safety?"

"Mrs. Ortiz, why don't we ensure that you or your husband can bring Selena to school and pick her up? That way, she is never alone and never waiting at the bus stops," said Mrs. Lipowski with concern.

"That will be fine. I feel much better about this," replied Mrs. Ortiz.

JIMMY AUGUST 1ˢᵗ 1969

Jimmy was allowed to go home after three weeks in protective custody. He was ordered to check in twice daily with Detectives Dillon and Valentine.

"Jimmy, we want you to lead your life normally. If Tony has a job for you, call the number on this business card before you go. Keep us constantly informed of where you go, when you leave, when you return, and your interactions with Tony and any of his men," said Detective Dillon, handing Jimmy his card.

"I will," said Jimmy. "I want my son and my family to be safe and Junie to be found and safe."

Jimmy left the station in a patrol car. The officer driving dropped him off at home.

Jimmy ran to the front door, and Maymie swung it open so hard it slammed into the door frame. She jumped into his arms and held onto him tightly.

"I was so worried about you, Jimmy. It's good you stayed in protective custody, but Clay and I missed you terribly!" Maymie exclaimed as she burst into tears.

"I missed you, too, May. I need to hold you for a few minutes," Jimmy said, grateful to be home.

"I'm helping the police. They asked me to continue my job with Tony, but I have to report to Detective Dillon twice a day."

Maymie said warily, "Oh, Jimmy, you have to be careful."

"I know," said Jimmy, "but nothing will stop me from finding Junie and who did this. And Tony knows that I will be working with Detective Dillon."

"May, where is that picture of Eddie with his friend?" asked Jimmy.

Maymie replied, "Right there on the mantel in the living room. Why?"

"I have to take the picture to the detectives at the police station. They are looking into the other man in the photo," said Jimmy.

"I remember him. I was just about nine or ten years old when he used to come around once in a while. I think his name was Ray. We called him Mr. Davis. He loved hearing my daddy's music at the old jazz club Tony used to run," Maymie said.

Jimmy asked, "Was he ever a police officer?"

Maymie replied, "Yes, I believe he still is. Almost ready to retire, I imagine."

Jimmy said, "May, could you go to the station and tell the detectives that? They are real nice and listen to everything I tell them."

"I guess so, Jimmy. If it will help, I'll go tomorrow," said Maymie.

The following day, Maymie called the number on Detective Dillon's business card, which he had given to Jimmy upon his release from custody. The number went directly to his desk.

"Hello, this is Detective Dillon."

"Um, Hello. This is Maymie Williams. I am calling about something Jimmy Barnes and I discussed last evening. Should I come over?"

Dillon replied, "Yes, when can you get here?"

"I can come in right after work, around 3 p.m.," said Maymie.

"That sounds good. I'll be here. Just ask for me at the main desk, and I'll come and get you. Don't say anything else to anyone here," cautioned Dillon.

"Should I bring the photo that you and Jimmy talked about? Maymie asked.

"Yes, bring that with you, but don't show it to anyone," Dillon instructed.

"All right, I will be there at 3 pm," said Maymie.

When Maymie returned home from work, she stuffed the framed photograph into her purse and headed to the police station.

Standing at the main desk, she asked the attending officer to let Detective Dillon know she was there.

In the background, behind the desk, Captain Burrows was eavesdropping.

The attending officer called Dillon's office to tell him Miss Williams was there for an appointment. Dillon appeared immediately and took her elbow, guiding her to his office.

"You didn't speak to anyone else?" asked Dillon.

"No, but I saw an officer in the back listening to me when I asked for you. I didn't recognize him, but he must have been a high-ranking officer from the look of his uniform."

"That must have been Captain Burrows," said Dillon, wondering why he was eavesdropping.

As they each sat, Dillon was behind the desk, and Maymie was in the straight-back leather chair in front of it.

Maymie began, "I brought the photo of Mr. Davis and my father." She handed it to Detective Dillon. "Does he look familiar to you?"

Dillion replied, "Yes, that is Officer Ray Davis. What can you tell me about him and his relationship with Tony Rossini and Jimmy?"

Maymie nervously said, "I know that Jimmy has been a drug runner for Tony. But I don't know about Tony's relationship with Ray Davis. Jimmy told me he sees Ray Davis sitting at the back booth in the diner almost every time he goes there. He said he didn't recognize him but knew he had seen him somewhere. Then we looked at this photograph. I also know that Ray Davis used to go to Tony's jazz nightclub before the incident with my father."

"Thank you, Miss Williams. Please continue," said Dillon.

"Well, Jimmy also told me he sees Ray Davis watching Rose when she is working the tables and counter at the diner. Jimmy thinks he sits in that back booth so no one will notice he is staring at Rose," replied Maymie. "Jimmy said it makes him feel strange when Ray stares at her."

"Jimmy also told me that he was in that booth the day Junie was kidnapped. He was there when Jimmy and Junie were getting milkshakes. Jimmy returned to the diner after Junie walked home, and Ray Davis was not in the booth. He believes Ray Davis might have something to do with Junie's disappearance." Maymie said apprehensively.

THE HOSPITAL AUGUST 8th 6:20 p.m. 1969

When they got the go-ahead, Detectives Dillon and Valentine headed to the hospital to question the girls.

"I'll go talk to June Williams," said Detective Valentine.

"I am going to check with the nurses to see who else is well enough to answer some questions," Detective Dillon told Valentine.

As Detective Valentine went into June's room, she saw Mrs. Williams and June hand in hand. June had just awakened from a short nap. Mrs. Williams gently stroked June's tiny hands and lightly brushed her hair from her forehead.

"Hello, Mrs. Williams. Would it be OK if I ask June a few questions?" asked Valentine. "I have all the notes from Officer Chase and just want to find out if there's anything else we can discover to help all these girls."

"Yes, Junie, do you mind speaking to Detective Valentine?" asked Mrs. Williams softly.

Detective Valentine was kind. Her mid-length copper hair was pulled back into a severe ponytail that hung loosely down to the middle of her back. Her porcelain, lightly freckled face had a broad, inviting smile, allowing June to relax and tell her story.

In a compassionate, gentle voice, Detective Valentine asked, "How are you feeling today, June?"

"Hi, Detective Valentine. I am so happy to be with my Mama and out of that disgusting place I was in for so long." June said assertively.

"I'm happy too, June. After reviewing all the notes from Officer Chase, I want to ask you a couple of questions about the people holding you and the other girls," said Valentine.

"OK," said June with a little swallow, looking at her mother as if asking for advice. Mrs. Williams nodded her head, assuring June that it was fine.

"June, do you know the names of the people who were keeping you in that place and what they looked like?" asked Valentine.

June replied, "The woman's name was DeeDee or Delores. They called her both, and she was the one in charge of us. She had blonde hair and was always dressed up in pretty dresses and jewelry. The man was a tall Black man with a deep voice. He looked a lot older than DeeDee."

June took a few minutes to breathe and continued. "His hair was white and short. He had darker skin than mine, and he seemed to know me. I didn't know him, except he looked like the man in the picture Mama has at home with my Daddy standing next to him."

"What kind of clothing did the men wear?" asked Valentine.

June replied, "The two men we saw the most both wore short-sleeved white shirts and dark blue pants with a big belt. They both had black shoes on. I didn't notice anything else. I thought it was strange that they dressed alike."

Valentine asked, "What did the man who came in to get Cinnamon look like?"

"He had a big stomach and bushy white hair that looked like a bird's nest to me. He was wearing overalls as if he had been working outside. But I saw that he wore a suit and tie under the overalls. I tried not to stare. I heard someone call him Moose, but I bet that wasn't his real name."

"Thank you, June. You've been extremely helpful," Detective Valentine said with a big smile. "We'll talk again soon."

"Bye," said June, waving to the detective. "Mama, she is so nice. Do you think I helped?"

"You sure did, Junie Bug," said Mrs. Williams, bursting with pride for her brave youngest child.

Detective Valentine went into the next room to talk to one of the recovering girls. "Hello, are you Sarah?" asked Valentine. "I'm Detective Valentine, and I am here to help find out what happened to all of you."

The weak, gaunt, dark-haired girl had bruises on her neck, face, and legs. She also had the most beautiful ocean blue eyes Detective Valentine had ever seen.

"Yes," said the girl weakly, "I'm Sarah. Am I in the hospital? Or are you here to take us somewhere again? I don't want to go. I hate that man. He hurts us!"

"No, Sarah, you're safe now. You are in the hospital and can recover here, and the nurses are very nice. Do you think you could answer a few questions?" asked Valentine gently.

"I think so. Is my mom here?" Sarah asked anxiously.

"Your mom is on her way. She is so relieved to know that we found you. Would you mind if one of the nurses sits with you while we talk?" asked Valentine, staying calm and assuring.

"Yes, I would like that, as long as my mom is on the way," said Sarah, pressing the button to sit up in her bed.

"She is definitely on the way. Thank you for allowing me to ask you a couple of questions, Sarah," Valentine told her.

Detective Valentine asked Sarah the same questions she had asked all the girls who could understand and remember. The main thread that pulled it together was Raymond, Delores, and a fat white man with white hair and overalls named Moose.

DETECTIVES AUGUST 8th 7:10 p.m. 1969

Detectives Dillon and Valentine met back at the station to compare information. Dillon had spoken to Maymie Williams, and Valentine had met with June Williams and Officer Chase.

"Shut the door," said Dillon to Valentine, "we need to speak quietly."

"What did you find out, Jack?" asked Detective Valentine.

"I got some great information from Maymie and the photograph from their home with Officer Davis and Eddie Williams," said Dillon.

"We definitely have something," said Valentine. "I spoke to June, Mrs. Williams, and some of the other rescued girls at the hospital. I have some damaging information about Ray Davis, and they all saw someone the adults called Moose."

"What?? That's big, he's our tipline guy," Dillon replied excitedly. "We'll call Tony Rossini and Officer Davis in to be questioned. If we don't get what we want from them, we'll hit them with the pictures and testimonies from the girls we interviewed."

As they spoke, Detective Dillon noticed Captain Burrows outside the office window.

"He sure fits June's description of the fat white man with white hair," said Detective Valentine. "Moose."

"Agreed," said Dillon. "And he always seems to be trying to

eavesdrop.”

“Let’s head over to the diner and talk to Tony Rossini. We’ll see where that leads,” said Dillon.

“It’ll have to wait until tomorrow morning. We'd better put a plan together so he doesn’t get too suspicious,” Valentine answered.

Dillon nodded in agreement.

TONY'S AUGUST 9th 10 a.m. 1969

Detectives Dillon and Valentine headed to Tony's Diner to interview him.

"Hello, Tony. Do you have a few minutes to answer some questions? Dillon asked.

"Detective Dillon, good morning," Tony replied as he turned to Stella.

"Stella, you and Rose take care of the customers. I will be in the office with Detectives Dillon and Valentine."

"OK, Tony," said Stella. "Not a problem. Rose will take the tables, and I'll hold down the counter."

Tony led the detectives to his office. Tony sat behind his desk, and the detectives sat across from him.

Detective Dillon began the conversation, "Tony, we need to find out the depth of your involvement with Ray Davis and possibly Captain Burrows in the abduction and assaults on the young girls we discovered in the shed on the farm property."

Valentine added, "We are aware of your 'side' business. We also know that you keep that side business private and pay for police protection to avoid trouble at the diner. We're not here to bust you for that, we are here for the truth."

Tony replied, "I can tell you that I've known Ray and his girlfriend, Delores, for several years."

Tony continued, "I knew Ray Davis and Delores were purchasing drugs from my guys. I don't know exactly what they did with those drugs, and I didn't ask. I don't deal in selling children, only in drugs and moving the money around. The drug money comes to me, and I pay my runners, and invest the rest."

Tony continued, "When I first heard of missing teens, I didn't suspect any of my guys or clients, and I didn't ask."

Detective Valentine asked, "Tony, what work does Jimmy Barnes do for you?"

"Jimmy is a junior runner for me. He makes sure orders get delivered to the right place, to the right people, and on time, and he is not allowed to ask any questions," Tony explained.

Valentine asked, "How do you know Officer Raymond Davis?"

"He was a regular customer at my jazz club in the late 50s and early 60s until Eddie Williams was attacked there in 1961," replied Tony, his demeanor changing to a sincerely sad look as he looked down and shook his head.

"What do you know about the attack and murder of Eddie Williams?" asked Detective Dillon.

Tony replied, "Eddie was a well-loved man, and no one seemed to have any grudges with him. I was shocked when I found him outside behind the club that night."

"Do you know who might have done this to him?" asked Dillon.

"I don't, said Tony. "It had all the signs of being a racial issue then. I didn't see anything except three men running away from the scene as I went outside to look for Eddie when he didn't come back in to get his tips and pay for that night."

"Two of the guys were white and one black, as far as I could tell. I only saw them from the back, and one of them turned around briefly, but I couldn't see his face. Ray wasn't one of them since he was inside the club with his girlfriend, Delores, that night," Tony clarified.

"Tony, how well do you know Captain Burrows at the CPD?" asked Dillon

"I've seen him here with his family once in a while. I've also seen him having lunch with Raymond Davis. They always sit in the last booth," said Tony. "Other officers come in for lunch meetings in that back booth, too. I have noticed that Ray is here almost daily."

Detective Valentine asked, "Do you ever notice Raymond Davis staring at or interacting with any of your staff other than to place an order?"

Tony answered, "He likes Rose Williams to be his waitress and asks for her. He likes to strike up a conversation with her, but I don't normally listen in. Eddie Williams and Ray Davis were great friends, so I never considered that unusual. He knows Mrs. Williams well, and so do I. The Williams are family to me."

"Thank you for your time, Tony," said Dillon. "We'll let you know if we have more questions. If you think of anything we need to know, call the station at the number on this card. It will go straight to my office."

Tony said, "Thanks, detectives. I want to figure this out as much as you do."

The detectives left Tony's office. After speaking briefly outside, they decided to go to the station to make notes and plan their next move.

MOOSE SEPT 1ˢᵗ 1969

John Burrows, a detective and commander in the CPD, was a massive, looming presence. He was not good-looking, with a puffy, round face, bushy white hair, a protruding, prominent nose, and a perpetually swollen lower lip—hence the nickname Moose. Raymond Davis worked closely with Burrows. John Burrows was a hard man to work for. His orders were chock-full of finding men of color and bringing them in for questioning regarding crimes in the city that went unsolved, making it appear that he was a champion at solving cases.

" I want you to bring in Jimmy Barnes about the young girls found in the machine shed," commanded Burrows, gesturing to the officer leaving on patrol. "Do it tomorrow after 10 p.m."

"Detectives Dillon and Valentine have questioned and released Mr. Barnes," answered the officer.

"I have not questioned him yet. Bring him in. Have Robinson pick him up," said Burrows, knowing that if Calvin Robinson picked him up, it wouldn't cause suspicion.

"Yes, sir," said the officer, afraid of the consequences of not following orders.

Officer Raymond Davis, listening to the conversation behind the door, needed to keep a low profile since the incident with Selena. The next evening, he radioed Officer Robinson, "Calvin, this is Ray. Captain Burrows is ordering you to bring Jimmy Barnes back here for more questioning."

Not wanting to question this, Officer Robinson replied, "OK, I'll head over there now." And as he turned his cruiser around to head to the Williams home, he had a sinking feeling that turned his stomach. He knew some things about Burrows.

Arriving at the Williams home at 10:30 p.m., Officer Robinson approached the front door and knocked. Jimmy answered.

"Hello, Officer Robinson, what can I do for you?" asked Jimmy nervously.

"Hello, Mr. Barnes. I was ordered to bring you to the station for more questioning." Officer Robinson stated. "You won't need to bring anything with you, and it shouldn't take too long."

Jimmy called to Maymie. "May, I have to go back for more questioning."

Maymie came to the door holding Clay and gave Jimmy a distressed look, "But it's so late. What could they possibly want at this hour?"

Officer Robinson led Jimmy to the patrol car. On the way to the station, Jimmy asked, "Do you know what they want? I told them everything, and it was all the truth," said Jimmy fearfully.

"I don't know, but keep being truthful, Mr. Barnes," replied Officer Robinson, not knowing what was in store for Jimmy.

JIMMY & BURROWS SEPT 2nd 1969

Arriving at the police station, Captain Burrows approached Jimmy and said, "Jimmy Barnes, come with me."

Jimmy felt highly despondent and fearful. This was not someone he knew well or trusted. Jimmy had heard rumors about Captain Burrows and was now about to experience it firsthand. Burrows was a foreboding presence, and Jimmy knew he had to tell him everything.

Burrows began in his blubbery, raspy, and booming voice, "So, Jimmy Barnes, what can you tell me about the disappearance of June Williams and the girls that were found in the machine shed at the farmhouse outside of the city?"

Jimmy went over everything he had told Dillon and Valentine. He told the truth. However, neither of the detectives was notified nor called into the office to inform them that Jimmy was being questioned again.

"Is that really the whole truth?" Burrows asked in a shifty tone.

"Yes, sir," said Jimmy honestly. "It is the entire truth."

"I know you're hiding something. What are you hiding?" asked Burrows accusingly, pulling himself closer to Jimmy's face. Burrows's size, grossly sweating with spittle in the corners of his mouth, was overbearing, leaning over Jimmy.

Jimmy stood his ground and looked Burrows in the eye, "I swear, nothing. I have nothing to hide," said Jimmy. "I already spoke to Detectives Dillon and Valentine."

"Well, Mr. Barnes, now you are speaking to me. And I know you're lying," claimed Burrows as he pounded an oversized fist on the table.

"No, sir, I am not lying," said Jimmy, who was beginning to feel the heavy pressure weighing him down. "I would not lie about my family."

"I'm going to hold you here until you can remember what the real truth is," Burrows stated commandingly.

"What? No, you have nothing to hold me on. My family is waiting for me at home, and I was released to go home," Jimmy pleaded loudly.

"Let's see if a couple of nights in a cell will jog your memory," Burrows said, not wavering and not listening to any weakness from Jimmy.

Burrows called for Lieutenant Rogers to get Jimmy. "Rogers, take Mr. Barnes to Cell number three. And no phone calls."

Lieutenant Rogers nodded, "Uh, yes, sir." But he shuddered at the thought of Jimmy going to Cell Three.

As Jimmy entered the cell, he noticed it was not the same as the one he was being held in for protective custody. This cell had stains on the walls, the floor, and the mattress. "What is that?" Jimmy thought as he walked in and sat on the only chair next to a metal desk attached to the wall.

Less than an hour later, Burrows entered the cell. "OK, Jimmy Barnes, let's talk."

DILLON 9:30 a.m. SEPT 3rd 1969

Detective Dillion's office phone rang at 9 a.m. on September 3rd. He had just entered his office carrying files of the girls who were found and files of the children still missing.

"Detective Dillon?" asked a woman's voice.

"Yes, who is this?" asked Dillon.

"Detective Dillon, this is Maymie Williams. Last night Jimmy was ordered to go to the police station for more questioning. I don't know why, and no one has called. Officer Robinson picked him up late last night, and he didn't come home. Can you help me?"

"Maymie, I had no idea. I will look into this immediately and see what is going on. May I call you when I have some news?" asked Dillon.

"Yes, of course. Thank you, I'm so worried," said Maymie with panic in her voice. "I've been up all night, terrified of what's happening."

Dillon put the files in a locked drawer and called Detective Valentine to help.

"Liz, we need to find out where Jimmy Barnes is. Maymie said Officer Robinson was ordered to pick him up late last night for more questioning, and he never came home. This sounds suspicious."

"OK, Jack, let's begin by finding out where he was taken and if Robinson knows anything. We'll look around here and see if anyone is in the holding cells."

"Let's go," Jack said, anxiously.

Dillon and Valentine walked to the hallway of cells. A few cells held wrongdoers with violations such as robbery, vehicle violations, DUI, and domestic violence, but nothing they didn't already know about.

As they walked the length of the hallway, they saw a locked door. The cell block number above the door said 'Cell 3'.

"Why is this locked?" asked Valentine. "I haven't seen this area before."

"I've never seen this cell," said Jack. I'll talk to the chief and the captain to find the key."

"I'll do a little more digging to see if any other prisoners know anything while you do that," said Valentine.

JIMMY & BURROWS 11:15 p.m. SEPT. 2ⁿᵈ 1969

"I told you everything I know. What more can I tell you?" asked Jimmy tying to not sound weak or defeated.

Burrows entered the cell after the other office staff had left for the day. Only the patrol officers remained that night. Two officers were at their desks while others were cruising their appointed rounds. Officer Davis was in the hallway so that Jimmy couldn't see him.

Burrows stood up so close to Jimmy he could feel his sweat and smell his shaky breath.

"Talk, Jimmy," ordered Burrows.

Jimmy looked up at Burrows and shook his head. "I have nothing new to report," claimed Jimmy with apprehension.

Burrows, who had his right hand behind his back, swung his fist into Jimmy's jaw and nose, drawing and spattering blood on the wall and all over Jimmy's clothing as Jimmy's head jerked back with such force he felt his neck would break.

Burrows' right fist was adorned with brass knuckles.

Jimmy sputtered and tried to talk, but was in shock and severe pain at this development.

"Talk!" shouted Burrows.

"I-I don't know what you want to know," Jimmy said sheepishly, sensing the thick stream and metallic taste of blood.

"You did this. You knew all about those girls in the shed and set June Williams up to be kidnapped. Confess now!" shouted Burrows, agitated and terrifying.

"No, I didn't! I didn't know anything about the shed and the girls. I love June Williams like a sister and would never set her up for danger," begged Jimmy.

Just as he spoke, Burrows pulled out his police nightstick and planted another shot into Jimmy's ribs, causing Jimmy to cry out, "STOP! What do you want?"

"I want your confession. I want the truth, then all of this stops," Burrows bellowed, raising his arm for another blow.

The beating went on for what seemed like hours. Jimmy was weaker and more confused. There was blood spatter on the walls and floor. Jimmy couldn't see, his eyes swollen and bleeding. Burrows pulled a cattle prod from a bag he had carried into the cell. Just as Jimmy looked up, Burrows hit him in the chest and stomach with the electric prod, throwing Jimmy backward onto the mattress. He then slid to the floor, slumped over, and prayed for this to stop.

"GET UP," barked Burrows.

Burrows grabbed Jimmy by his shirt to pull him up and held the electroshock prod to his genitals and then to his chest.

Jimmy's head drooped, blood streaming from his mouth, eyes, face, and ears. Captain Burrows thrust Jimmy back into the chair violently, carelessly, as he got as close as possible to his face.

"Now, Jimmy, my boy, tell me what I want, and you can make all of this stop." Burrows laughed a sinister belly laugh, enjoying this with great enthusiasm.

Officer Davis walked up to look in the cell. Jimmy saw him, and his fear heightened. Officer Davis looked as if he might say something to Burrows, but he remained silent and could only stare helplessly at this situation. Another officer followed behind Davis. He backed away, head down, having the same reaction. No one would help Jimmy, and no one wanted to be next.

Jimmy, barely breathing, said, "I confess, I did it. "I don't know what I did, but I did it."

"OK," said Burrows as he handcuffed Jimmy to the radiator and pushed him onto the filthy, blood-stained mattress on the floor. "I'll send in a medic to patch you up, and then you're going to prison."

Jimmy was in so much pain and filled with so much fear that he couldn't move or speak. He fell back onto the dirty mattress and whispered, "Maymie..." barely getting enough air to make any words, just moans.

Burrows left the station after writing up the confession and forcing Jimmy to sign it. Jimmy's hands were barely able to hold a pen. Lieutenant Rogers heard the whole encounter. When Burrows left for the night, Lieutenant Rogers called Detective Dillon to meet with him. It was almost 1 a.m., and Dillon was not in his office. It would have to wait until later, hoping that Jimmy survived the night.

This was not the first time Captain Burrows had turned to torture to coerce a false confession, especially from a man of color.

CELL #3 11 a.m. SEPT. 3rd 1969

Lieutenant Rogers entered his office quietly, calling Detectives Dillon and Valentine to meet him privately.

As the two detectives entered Lieutenant Rogers' office, the Lieutenant locked the door and pulled the blinds. He knew no one would question that, since it was normal when he was in a meeting.

"Jack and Liz, I need your help." Lieutenant Rogers handed Dillon a key. "This key opens cell block number three. I have it on good authority that Captain Burrows is torturing men into false confessions. No one knows that I have this key, so be sure to keep it safe and hidden."

Rogers continued, "Burrows is out all day today until late this evening. I would like you to investigate what is happening in that cell. I have seen the cell empty. It's filthy, but I had not seen anyone in the cell until last night. Captain Burrows ordered Jimmy Barnes to be brought in again for more questioning. I was in my office, but Burrows had no idea I was there. I'm afraid Mr. Barnes was tortured and abused to sign a confession stating that he was the one who kidnapped June Williams."

"No wonder Maymie called," Dillon said. "Jimmy's wife called to tell me he hadn't come home last night after Officer Robinson picked him up."

"That cell is pretty soundproof because of the solid steel, heavy locking door. Once it is opened, the only bars are at eye level and are window-sized. This key opens that second door, too. However, I heard part of the interrogation, and it was nothing I could ever imagine happening here. Jimmy needs to be in a hospital. He falsely confessed to the kidnapping, and Burrows made him sign a written confession. Burrows wrote the confession, not Jimmy." Rogers said, stating the facts.

"We'll go check it out. Is this a good time? I assume there is no one around that area at this time," asked Dillon.

"Yes, go now, and I can intervene with any nosy cops," said Lieutenant Rogers.

Detective Dillon took the key and put it into his front pocket. Detective Valentine looked at Dillon, ready but braced to see what was happening there.

They went to Cell #3, avoiding the calls and noise from the other offenders in other cells. One man in a cell on the left side of the hall went to the bars and whispered to Valentine, " Hey, Burrows is bad news, and I think he might have beaten that poor guy to death last night."

Valentine nodded at the man and put one finger to her lips as if to say, "Be quiet." The man nodded back and kept watching. The man whispered, "Catch that son of a bitch."

JIMMY NOON SEPT. 3rd 1969

As soon as Dillon unlocked the heavy door and slid it open, they saw Jimmy Barnes at death's door, his arm handcuffed to the radiator. Dillon quietly rushed to his side as Valentine watched the door and the hallway.

"Jimmy, Jimmy, look at me," said Dillon, gently tapping Jimmy's leg.

"Does he have a pulse?" asked Valentine nervously.

Carefully touching Jimmy's carotid artery, Dillon felt a weak pulse.

"Liz, we have to get him to the hospital. He has a weak pulse, and he is not breathing well and can't speak. Get Lieutenant Rogers and call for an ambulance," Dillon said urgently.

"Be right back," Liz said.

Lieutenant Rogers called for an ambulance, which arrived in less than ten minutes.

Jimmy was lifted onto a plank board and cautiously hoisted into the ambulance.

"Before Burrows gets here, we have to contact the DA," said Valentine. She continued, "It's evident that the written confession is false. We will get to the bottom of this. I am certain that Jimmy is not the first man to be tortured into a false confession in that cell."

"Lieutenant Rogers, are there more abuse cases involving Burrows?" asked Dillon discreetly.

"Rumors. This is the first time I have seen it in action," explained Lieutenant Rogers. "But I will be turning over every stone to make this stop."

"We will question any of the other cellmates to see what they know," Dillon said as he handed the Cell #3 block key back to Lieutenant Rogers.

"Liz, let's head to the Williams home to speak to Maymie and Mrs. Williams, then to the hospital for information on Jimmy's condition."

"This is incomprehensible," Valentine said empathetically.

As the detectives left the station, Lieutenant Rogers called the DA's office to set up an emergency meeting.

District Attorney Michael Levine set up a meeting between the detectives and the Lieutenant for September 4th at 9 a.m. in his office at the courthouse.

As Detectives Dillon and Valentine entered the courthouse, Lieutenant Rogers was waiting for them. DA Levine walked to the lobby to meet them and walk them to his office.

"Thank you all for meeting with me. Lieutenant Rogers has briefed me. Detectives Dillon and Valentine, do you have anything you want to add?" asked DA Levine.

"Has Burrows done anything like this before?" asked Dillon.

"We've been investigating him for a few years. He is alleged to have been involved in other instances of corruption in the police department. We need to speak to eyewitnesses or catch him in the act to uncover the facts. It sounds like we're closer," said DA Levine. He continued, "It doesn't happen with just one guy. My guess is that more officers are involved in this."

"We're investigating the corruption in his department. We have information on his alleged dealings in drugs, trafficking, and department corruption," said Valentine. This may even date back to the early 60s and the murder of Eddie Williams."

As the meeting continued, Lieutenant Rogers confirmed, "Officer Raymond Davis is likely involved and has been working with or for Burgess. I've been keeping track of car 247 and when it's checked out and back in. I'm witnessing some significant discrepancies in the time frames."

"Lieutenant Rogers, you heard the scuffle going on in Jimmy Barnes' cell, did you see anything?" asked DA Levine.

"Yes, I saw Burgess take Mr. Barnes to the cell to interview him about his missing family member, June Williams. Jimmy Barnes had already been questioned and cleared by Detectives Dillon and Valentine."

He continued, "They took Mr. Barnes to Cell #3, a solitary confinement cell. A special key is needed to open the sliding iron door and the cell door."

"Right," said Dillon. "When we went in to see Jimmy, he had been brutally attacked and was handcuffed to a radiator in the cell. His condition was bad. The hospital told us he had severe injuries to his head, neck, eyes, nose, mouth, chest, and knees, and he had blistering burns on the arm that was handcuffed to the radiator."

“Would you testify to this in court?” asked DA Lavine.

“I would,” said Dillon.

“I would as well,” confirmed Valentine.

“Our next step is to speak with Tony Rossini. He may be able to help us unravel more of the pieces of the information we have,” said DA Lavine. “Can I count on you as well, Lieutenant? Keeping this information quiet will go a long way in the prosecution.”

“Yes, I am willing to testify,” said Lieutenant Rogers.

JIMMY 1970

Jimmy spent more than five months in the hospital and eight more weeks at home recovering from his injuries inflicted by John Burrows while being held unlawfully and tortured. With the help of his family, the Williams family, he was released from the hospital in time for January and the new year of 1970.

The Williams family spent long days and nights recovering from the series of events, including the death of Eddie Williams, the abduction of June, and the abuse and false confession of Jimmy Barnes.

June had night terrors and night sweats several nights a week. Jimmy suffered from post-traumatic stress. Mrs. Williams, Denice, Maymie, and Rose held their family together with compassion, love, and understanding.

These acts of injustice and the subsequent developments never once led the family to waver in their love for each other. They became stronger and were able to fight harder for injustices of all kinds.

Detectives Dillon and Valentine, along with Lieutenant Rogers and DA Lavine, continued to investigate why this happened, how long it had been going on, how it kept growing unnoticed by authorities, and who was behind all of the crimes, including information on the kidnapping and abuse of the missing teens, the homicide of Julie Langdon, the drugging and maliciousness of the violations and the harm of the captured teens, and where and how it all started. Now that they had a good idea of everyone involved, it was time to plan arrests.

These investigations led them back to 1961 and the senseless, horrific homicide of Eddie Williams.

It was discovered that Raymond Davis and John Burrows hired two men and planned the attack on Eddie. John Burrows was the lead in the planned beating and stabbing of Eddie. John Burrows sliced off two of Eddie's fingers to steal his pinky ring. Tony Rossini had no prior knowledge of the planning or the attack.

John Burrows was a junior detective from 1960 to 1961. He aimed to advance in the ranks and become the department's captain. In 1968, he was promoted to Chicago Police Detective after serving as a ruthless military investigator in Vietnam.

After giving a false confession under torture, with a paperclip he found on the floor, Jimmy Barnes scratched messages into the paint in the cell. The messages are evidence that Mr. Barnes's confession was obtained through the use of torture. He scratched a message onto the metal bench along the wall: 'Police threaten me with violence. Hit and burned me, suffocated me with plastic. No lawyer or phone call. Signed false statement to kidnapping, murder.'

Jimmy Barnes was photographed after he was tortured. Those photographs corroborated a medical examination of Mr. Barnes.

COURT TRIAL JANUARY 1972

A little over a year after John Burrows, while using a nickname of Moose, was implicated and indicted of abducting and abusing teens, he was found guilty of lying about "directly participating in or implicitly approving the torture" of at least 21 people – men and women of color, in police custody to force false confessions over four or more years. John Burrows and officers under his command were believed to have targeted communities of color, kidnapping and torturing individuals, producing confessions to crimes they did not commit.

It was discovered that Moose is Captain Burrows. He owns the farmhouse, the machine shed, and the cornfield property. He abducted Julie Langdon as she rode her bicycle on the road by his farmhouse in 1966. He then threw her bicycle into the cornfield, where it was found by a farmhand. Police came to collect the bike and put it into police storage. Police ran an ad in a community newspaper with a photo of the purple bicycle to find out whose it was. Nothing else was investigated.

Captain Burrows rented his farmhouse and shed to Raymond Davis and Delores Ryan. They supplied him with drugs to keep the young girls quiet and compliant.

Burrows lied on the stand about his involvement in the torture, kidnapping, and trafficking.

DA Levine held strong with trial testimonies from Tony Rossini, Detectives Dillon and Valentine, Jimmy Barnes, Maymie Williams,

June Williams, and Mrs. Pearl Williams.

Former police captain John Burrows was held on charges of kidnapping, rape, child trafficking, drug trafficking, child abuse, and murder. Lesser charges were robbery and corruption. Raymond Davis and John Burrows were also charged with police brutality and first-degree murder in the case of Eddie Williams in 1961.

Delores Ryan was charged with child abuse, kidnapping, trafficking, and being an accessory to murder in the cases of Eddie Williams and Julie Langdon.

Burrows, Raymond Davis, and Delores (DeeDee) Ryan were all arrested and held for sentencing.

During his testimony, Jimmy Barnes stated,

"He tried to kill me. It left a hollow, ripping feeling that's always there. I can't ever shake it. I don't sleep because it happens all over again when I close my eyes."

Jimmy continued with tears in his eyes, "I shouldn't have let Burrows do that to me, but there was nothing I could do. I kept thinking how I could get out of it, but there was nothing I could do—absolutely nothing. There was nothing to say, nowhere to go. I remember looking around the room at two other officers who were watching. I thought one of them would say something like 'that's enough, stop', but they never did."

All were found guilty on all charges, and sentencing was set for March 30th, 1972. Burrows and Davis received life without the possibility of parole, while Delores Ryan received a seven-year sentence.

For his testimony and honesty, Tony Rossini was put on probation for three years and ordered to cease his drug business. He was allowed to keep the boxing gym and the diner. He was also ordered to donate a portion of the drug money he had accumulated to the Department of Children and Family Services, the Child Protective Services of Chicago, and the foster care program.

After the trials, the man's pinky ring with the initials EWII was returned to Mrs. Williams. Detectives Dillon and Valentine had it cleaned and put it into a red jewelry box. They presented it to her in a small ceremony just for the family at the police station. Mrs. Williams held it to her chest, and her eyes filled with tears of joy, love, and loss.

"I can never thank you enough for all you have done for our family. I am blessed," said Mrs. Williams with relief and happiness.

The Williams family embraced and shook hands with the detectives and the officers.

"We are so happy we were there to help you. Thank you for standing up for your family and the other families of missing children," said Lieutenant Rogers with admiration.

APRIL 1971

Although Rose's older sisters wanted to attend college and develop careers, they had families to raise now. Rose's dreams of becoming a lawyer intensified and reinforced as she watched her family live on low wages and work so hard to make ends meet.

Everyone pitched in to bank some money for Rose to attend college and law school. She worked at the diner until graduation, earning good tips and an hourly wage. Since Tony was part of the family, he ensured Rose got good tables with big tippers.

"Mr. Tony, do you have a few minutes to talk?" asked Rose.

"Yes, I do, Rose, anything for you," Tony said graciously.

"I'm going to be leaving for college soon. I want to ask if you could write a letter of recommendation for me to Howard University in DC," said Rose. She continued, "My goal is to attend Law School after completing my undergraduate degree. You've always been so good to our family, like an uncle. It would mean a lot to me."

Tony said, "Rose, I'm happy for you, but I'm also sorry to see you leave your job. You're one reason the customers come in. Most of them always ask for you. But I know you are growing up and want to become who you were meant to be. So, yes, I will be more than happy to help you get there. When do you need your letter?"

"Oh, thank you, Mr. Tony!" exclaimed Rose. "I have to send it out next week if possible."

"OK, I will get it to you by Friday," assured Tony.

Rose was ecstatic: "I'm so excited. I would still love to work here whenever I can, like on breaks and holidays. Possibly over the summers until I can intern at a law office."

"That would make everyone very happy, Rose. Especially our customers," replied Tony.

Mrs. Williams was unwaveringly proud of her daughters, who all graduated from high school with good grades. But she cried happy tears when she was notified that Rose had won a scholarship to attend the University of her choice, with everything paid for except for books.

Rose won the scholarship for her academics, high grade point average, participation in community service organizations helping underprivileged kids who were at risk for juvenile delinquency, and after-school programs to help kids read and do better at math. Mrs. Williams knew Rose had been busy and working extremely hard, but this took her entirely by surprise.

When she called Rose to come into the living room so she could tell her, the words wouldn't come out. She handed Rose the letter from the school.

"Your daddy would be so proud." Mrs. Williams said as Rose took the letter.

As Rose read the letter, her excitement bubbled over. She jumped up and down, holding the letter in one hand and waving the other in the air, cheering and whooping. Denice, who was home from work then, ran into the room and began to jump and cheer.

"What are we cheering for?" Denice asked, amused.

Rose handed her the letter. Denice let go of a muffled shriek since her other hand covered her open mouth.

"Oh, Rose, I am so proud of you! Let's have a party!"

Mrs. Williams, sitting now, said, "Yes, a party!"

The neighbors below the Williams ran up to see if everything was OK. Rose exclaimed, "OK? YES, Everything is coming up…well…ROSES!!"

They filled the neighbors in on what had transpired. As word spread about the fantastic news, party planning was in motion.

In September 1971, the Flower Girls made a pact to get tattoos of their flower name, each on the top of their left foot. They had been friends since meeting in the fifth grade, and now, as they planned their bright futures, this gesture would deepen the extraordinary bond they had built over the years, which was now cemented in beauty and spirit, and their connection as lifelong friends and family.

CELEBRATION MAY 1972

Everyone was invited to The Flower Girls' graduation party, which was held in the basement of the church that the Williams family attended. The weather was beautiful: perfect clear blue skies, a light breeze, and bright sunshine. It was a celebration of accomplishment and healing.

All the families helped decorate for the occasion with flowers, banners, and regalia in their high school colors of gold, royal blue, and white. A long table was full of cards and gifts.

Alice and her family were included in the festivities because they were like family. Mr. and Mrs. Russell were proud of Alice and her friends for standing up for each other and always doing what was right for everyone.

The party food was abundant. Mrs. Williams made ham and roast beef sandwiches on her homemade buns. She also made her famous chocolate whipped cream dessert, which everyone requested. Gerald and Jimmy barbequed the chicken and ribs that Tony donated.

Iris's dad brought his famous Irish potato salad. Mrs. O'Brien made Irish Soda Bread with chocolate chips. Lily's mom made her special Japanese finger cookies and a massive cake with flowers, all made from colorful frosting. The cake was stunning. It had a red rose at the top surrounded by a pink and white Stargazer lily with bright pink dots on one side and a bright purple iris on the other.

The neighbors and friends who helped with decorations asked Mrs. Sato where she got the cake. When she told them she made it, everyone asked if she took orders for special occasion cakes. She hid a soft chuckle with one hand over her mouth as she blushed. It was a proud day for her and the other parents.

Alice and her parents brought Alice's favorite French carrot salad, Chex Mix, and a Key Lime pie for dessert.

Photos of the Flower Girls from the day they met to this current graduation gala were on a giant poster board for everyone to see. The crowd favorite was a photo of all three Flower Girls entering the sixth grade. They had their arms around each other and the biggest smiles anyone had ever seen. It was a prediction that nothing could ever happen to keep them apart.

Music played through a small boombox, including Sam Cooke, Marvin Gaye, The Four Tops, Smokey Robinson, Diana Ross, The Temptations, and more. Dancing, laughing, and reminiscing went on throughout the evening. Iris, Lily, and Rose felt like movie stars.

As always, the Williams sisters danced and laughed as everyone joined in.

Someone tapped a spoon on a glass to call attention to a special gift.

Tony Rossini announced that he was donating something unique to each graduate.

He donated $500 to Rose for her dedication and goal of attending law school. To Lily, he donated a brand-new high-tech Olympus OM-1 camera so she could keep striving to be the best in journalism and photographing scenes to help solve crimes.

To Iris, he donated money to fund a one-year scholarship at the crisis center to mentor children and families to help pull themselves out of their downtrodden situations, and to help women in domestic violence situations.

Tony announced, "Without these young women and their families, I don't know where I would be. I know they have made my life more meaningful and full up to the brim."

Everyone stood and applauded as Tony opened his arms as if to hug the entire community.

GRADUATION DAY 1972

On Sunday, June 4th, 1972, the Flower Girls donned their royal blue caps and gowns with gold trim for the graduation ceremony. Everyone in the Williams family was there, smiling from ear to ear. Seated together were Denice, Gerald, and Pearl; Maymie, Jimmy, and Clay; June and Mrs. Williams. They sat hand in hand as the Satos and the O'Briens sat next to them, with Alice's parents next to the Satos.

Max and Selena were in attendance with the Ortiz family, including Sebastian. Officer Robinson was invited but could not attend due to his patrol schedule.

The three proud graduates wore matching white sandals under their graduation gowns, which were paired with summer dresses in shades of lemon yellow, pale lavender, and cotton candy pink. Everyone commented on the beautiful tattoo artwork on the tops of their feet. They all looked exquisitely put together and so grown-up.

"Where have our little girls gone? Mrs. O'Brien asked, reminiscing.

"They grew up in a flash. Our beautiful daughters," said Mrs. Sato, leaning her head to Mrs. O'Brien.

The mothers all wiped tears of joy, and the men in the families sat upright, arms crossed with so much pride it looked like their hearts would burst right out of their chests.

After the ceremony, everyone met at the park for an evening of hugs, pride, and tales of three girls named after flowers. As the evening passed, and the teens were all sitting in a circle sharing stories of their school days, Officer Robinson drove by on his usual patrol, and the teens ran over to him to thank him for all he had done over the years to help them get through life and tragedy.

He wished them well on their adventures after high school and asked all the graduates where they were headed and what direction their lives would take.

Before he drove away, he motioned for Jimmy to come over and speak to him.

"Jimmy, how are you doing? Are you recovering well?" asked Officer Robinson.

"I'm feeling almost back to normal. I've been working on running and doing some lifting. Tony has me in his boxing gym three days a week, and it's hard, but I'm getting stronger all the time. Thanks for checking on me," replied Jimmy with respect and sincerity.

"I have something I'd like to propose to you soon. Something that might change your life," said Robinson.

"I'm interested. Fill me in," said Jimmy.

"I'm putting a plan in motion to make some big changes in our community, and you can be part of it. I'll speak to you early next year when it's all set in motion," Robinson told Jimmy.

"I'm looking forward to it. Thanks again, man," said Jimmy as he waved to Officer Robinson and headed back to the party in the park.

ROSE MOVES TO DC

Rose was accepted into the pre-law program at Howard University in Washington, DC. She would leave for Howard in August of 1972 to begin her undergraduate degree.

"My dream is coming true," Rose said to Mrs. Williams. "Mama, I am so excited I can't sleep or even eat. I'm going to miss you and our family so much. I can't believe I won't see Lily and Iris every day."

Mrs. Williams held Rose's hands in hers. Looking into her eyes, she said, "Rose, I am so proud of you. I want to shout it to the heavens."

Rose's eyes swelled with happy, excited tears as she hugged her mother close. "Mama, we've been through a lot the past few years. But now, it's all coming together so joyfully."

Throughout the summer, the Flower Girls spent as much time together as they could, swimming, biking, and walking, having a wonderful last summer together before college.

Lily carried her new Olympus OM-1 camera everywhere she went. She was learning how to take clear photos of people, landscapes, and small things she found on the sidewalks and beach at Lake Michigan.

Iris always carried a notebook, noting how she might be able to help the people around her. Whenever she thought of something, she wrote it down. Helping kids at the community center showed her that helping others and her time are the best things she could offer to those in need. She spent a few hours a week working with the kids at the community center and the foster care office while she learned what her role could be in helping change lives.

Rose studied trial transcripts from the library. She instinctively knew that this was what she was meant to do. She had a summer meeting with DA Levine and helped in his office twice weekly. He said he would always be there to help her learn so that law school would be a breeze. Although they both knew it was not going to be a breeze. Rose was ready for the challenge, and she embraced it.

When August first rolled around, Rose was packed and ready to take the train to Washington, DC. Lily and Iris would stay close and attend The University of Chicago. The families met at Union Station for a tearful and joyful farewell.

"Rose, I'll miss you terribly! I can't wait for our first holiday break so we can all be together," Iris said, contemplating Thanksgiving and Christmas together.

"Me too," said Lily. "What are we going to do without your face every day? I love you so much."

The Flower Girls gave each other a big group hug. Then they all waved, blowing kisses to Rose as she checked her suitcase and boarded the train.

"See you soon, Rose," said June, waving and reaching out to hug her harder.

"Yes, see you soon!" the girls exclaimed.

Mrs. Williams's tears began to trickle down both cheeks. "Are you

OK, Mama?" asked June wrapping her arms around her mother's waist.

"Yes, little one, I am just fine," said Mrs. Williams as she held her youngest close. "I'm so proud of Rose and all of you girls. You have grown up to be strong and independent."

Rose's mind wandered on the train as she sat stoically, not letting anyone see her jittery hands while riding the bus. Rose could no longer hold it in as she felt her eyes starting to burn, tasting salty tears streaming down her cheeks to her lips.

She put her head down and quietly sobbed. "Oh, Daddy, I'm really doing it! I'm doing it for you, Mama, and our family. I'm excited and scared all at the same time. But I got this. I am making it happen!"

This was why she had saved every penny and why she was going to law school after college. Rose imagined herself in a courtroom, prosecuting those who hurt her family and others and obtaining justice for all victims and their families.

A NEW BEGINNING

Rose and her mother visited Howard University after she was accepted during her senior year. The University helped her find a small but efficient apartment on campus. She had one roommate named Elenor. They met over the summer and were both excited to begin school.

Elenor, a striking woman from the West Indies who was raised in Michigan, was also in undergraduate school for pre-law. She was tall, thin, and athletic, with smooth caramel skin and shoulder-length dark hair with a mind of its own. She wore her hair in artistic braids or loose with just a long scarf as a headband tied at the side, flowing over one shoulder.

Elenor previously had an offer to play on the West Indies Women's Cricket Team but chose to attend an American University and study law. This made it great for working together on assignments and understanding their courses.

Rose was very serious. She did not go out much or party. She wanted to study and be sure her grades got her to the top of the class and entry into the School of Law. Elenor seemed fine with finishing her work and then going out with friends.

A few weeks into the first semester, Elenor asked Rose if she would like to meet a friend of hers, Franklin. "Franklin is a nice guy with ambitions in the medical field, and he's a year older," said Elenor. "And he is very handsome," Elenor added with a grin.

"Ummm, sure, I'd like to meet him," Rose said, thinking for a moment. She thought it might be nice to meet some men on campus who were serious about doing something to help others and moving their lives in a forward direction.

"Wonderful," said Elenor. "I don't think having him come over here is a good idea, but how about meeting at the coffee stand by the main building tomorrow after our 11 o'clock class?"

Rose said, "Yes, that sounds like a good plan."

"OK, I'll let him know," Elenor said happily.

"What should I wear?" thought Rose. She looked at everything in her closet, which wasn't much, and chose a light fall sweater in pumpkin orange and her flared jeans with embroidered wildflowers in many colors around the bottom that her mother bought for her before she left for DC.

"This will work!" she said. "I will look casual but nice."

She met Elenor at the coffee stand after class, and they sat at one of the picnic tables in the campus courtyard.

"How do I look?" asked Rose.

"You look beautiful. That color brings out your eyes!" said Elenor. "Oh, there's Franklin," she said, waving for him to join them.

Franklin walked over to the table and sat down. "Frank, please meet Rose."

"Hello, Franklin," said Rose, offering to shake his hand.

"Hello, Rose," said Franklin, taking her up on her handshake.

The trio talked about their University experience since starting the semester a couple of months ago and seemed very comfortable with each other.

Rose looked at her new-ish Timex watch with the fake green snakeskin band, "OOO, I better get going! Humanities is my next class in about ten minutes."

Surprised at the time, Elenor said, "Wow, time sure went fast. OK, let's run. See you later, Frank."

Franklin said, "See you later, El. Rose, may I see you later, too?"

Rose and Elenor smiled. Rose said, "Yes, I'd like that."

IRIS AND LILY FALL 1972

Walking the campus to the dining hall at The University of Chicago, Iris asked Lily, "Have you seen Officer Robinson patrolling lately?"

"Not since our graduation," said Lily contemplatively. "I was just mentioning that to Alice. Do you think he got the promotion he was working towards?"

"Maybe, I hope so. He helped us a lot through our high school years," replied Iris as they returned their trays and walked out together.

"See you at the library to study in a couple of hours," Lily called to Iris.

"Yes, see you there," said Iris, waving to Lily, noticing how beautiful the trees were becoming.

As they headed to classes, Lily instinctively decided to call Rose to check on her after they got back to their dorm room.

Lily gathered her change and stopped at the payphone on the east side of the dorm housing where she and Iris lived. She dialed the operator and asked to make a long-distance call to Howard University student housing apartments, then gave the number to the operator. She dropped some coins into the slots on the phone for the number of minutes she wanted to speak to Rose.

The phone in Rose's apartment rang twice before she heard a voice on the other end of the line say, "Hello, this is Rose Williams."

Lily was ecstatic to hear Rose's voice.

"Rose, this is Lily. How are you doing? I miss you so much!"

Rose said joyfully, "Lily! I love that you are calling! How are you and Iris?"

"We're both doing great. We're meeting at the library in an hour, and I wanted to call to see how things are in DC," said Lily, delighted to hear Rose's voice.

"Well," Rose said, "I met a guy. He's adorable and very charming. Polite and sweet, too. His name is Franklin Harris."

"This is exciting," said Lily. "I can't wait to hear more. How are your classes and your roommate?"

Rose replied, "I love all of my classes so far. Elenor is a fun roommate and a good study partner. She loves going out every Friday night, but I don't do that. I'd rather relax and study. She introduced me to Franklin."

"We miss you a ton," said Lily. "We'll be together over the holidays in just a couple of months. Iris and I cannot wait! Alice and I are so happy together, and Iris is dating someone, but I'll let her tell you about that."

"I miss you both very much," Rose said. "I can't wait to get together and hug you both when we get home for Thanksgiving and Christmas!"

They both sent their love to each other, and the call ended. Lily went to her room and waited for Iris to finish her class so they could meet at the library.

ROSE AND ELENOR NOVEMBER 1972

The Flower Girls made plans to meet at the Williams's house once they were home for the holiday break. They planned to go Christmas shopping, mostly window shopping, and have meals together to catch up.

Elenor talked Rose into going out with her Friday night before they left for the holiday break.

"Well, OK," Rose said, contemplating, "That would be fun."

"It will be the first time you've gone out with me. I want to introduce you to a boy I have been seeing for a few weeks. His name is Tommy, Tommy D. Stone, and he is so cute. His friends call him TD since his middle name is Davis," Elenor said to Rose. She continued, "He lives off campus and works at a construction site for his father."

"Is he a nice guy?" asked Rose.

"So far, he is a gentleman. We like to talk about our lives, my studies, and where our lives are heading. He is usually pretty quiet and lets me do most of the talking. But he always seems to listen," said Elenor.

"Have you kissed him?" asked Rose.

"Well...yes. He is a good kisser," Elenor said with a shy giggle.

"I can't wait to meet the guy who's making your heart flutter," said Rose, "I want to see if he's good enough for you!"

"Friday at 7 p.m., we'll meet up at the Half Shot Pub off campus. I told him all about you," Elenor said with a gleeful mini dance.

"Sounds good to me," said Rose. "I think I will invite Franklin."

"Surprise," said Elenor. "I already did. I was hoping you'd want to come out for a fun Friday night."

They laughed and talked as they enthusiastically walked back to their apartment, anticipating a fun weekend before heading home until January.

Friday was a flurry of packing for home and getting ready to go out on the town for Rose and Elenore. They tried on each other's clothing and decided that Elenore would wear Rose's off-white peasant blouse that was light, loose, and tied at the neckline. It was adorned with embroidered bluebells and light green leaves.

Elenore's prairie skirt was the same shade of blue—or close enough to match the blouse. She wore dark brown faux leather platform boots, a long multi-colored scarf around her neck and shoulders, a blue and brown headband, and large gold hoop earrings.

"Oh, Elenore, you look just beautiful! Your makeup is perfect, and I love my blouse on you," Rose said as Elenore twirled in front of the full-length mirror on the back of the bathroom door.

"Let's get you dressed," Elenore said to Rose as they giggled and found themselves immersed in excitement.

Rose decided on her favorite hip-hugger bell-bottom jeans, a lightweight black turtleneck sweater, and Elenore's red, gold, and blue embroidered vest. Her shoes were beige high-top boots with embroidered flowers in red, yellow, blue, and pink from the toes to the rim that laced up and tied at the top. She wore electric blue triangle-shaped earrings that hung from her ears, accentuating her long, perfect neckline, and her hair was styled in a natural, loose afro. Her silky blue head scarf was tied perfectly, so it floated over one shoulder.

"WOW, you look spectacular," Elenore told Rose. "I'm so excited for you to meet Tommy. I hope I don't trip and fall in these platform boots tonight! She said, laughing.

"Ready to go?" asked Elenore.

"Ready and willing," replied Rose.

The roommates grabbed their jackets and purses and left arm in arm.

It took them about ten minutes to walk to the Half Shot Pub. As they walked, tons of students were headed to the row of bars and pubs just off campus for a fun Friday night. This was exhilarating for Rose as they waved to everyone they knew.

They got to the pub and met Franklin outside. "Wow, you ladies sure know how to turn heads! You are beautiful," exclaimed Franklin, enchanted by the sight of these two women.

Rose and Elenore curtseyed and giggled.

"Have you seen Tommy?" asked Elenore.

"I think he is already inside. Let's go in," said Franklin.

Inside, it was loud and exciting. Rose had never gone out to have this kind of fun all semester. There was loud music and so many people. It looked like a sea of dancers bobbing up and down in perfect waves of synchronicity.

"I'm so glad you talked me into going out, Elenore." Rose was ecstatic and had to yell over the crowd and music, but loved it.

"This is going to be a night to remember," Elenore proclaimed. "Let's order something at the bar."

"I've got this round, ladies," said Franklin.

ELENORE 11p.m. NOV. 17th 1972

Rose felt tired and knew she had to catch the bus to Chicago the following day. She pulled Elenore aside and said, "Elenore, I'm going to call it a night and walk back to the apartment. I have to catch the bus tomorrow. Are you ready to go home, too?"

"Not quite yet," replied Elenore. "Tommy wants to go to the bar across the street for a bit, so I'll go with him over there. He has a car and can drive me home, so I'll be home around midnight. Is Franklin going to walk home with you?"

"He's going to go as far as his place, then I'll go the rest of the way by myself. I'll be fine," Rose confirmed. "Don't forget your purse at the bar, and be careful. I want to hear all about you and Tommy when you get home, so wake me up."

"I can't wait to tell you about the night and hear about yours!" said Elenore excitedly.

Rose waved, then pulled on her tan suede fringed jacket, and Franklin extended his arm for her to take.

"Rose, I really like being with you. I'm heading to my parents' house in South Carolina for the holiday break, but I can't wait to see you in January. May I call you at your mother's house over the break?"

"Yes, of course," said Rose. "I would like that."

The two walked arm in arm until they reached Franklin's building. "This is my building," said Franklin.

"It sure is," said Rose.

Franklin took Rose's face gently in his hands to kiss her. She had been waiting for this moment. She put her hands on his wrists as he leaned into her, and they kissed for the first time. Rose blushed, and her head dropped so he couldn't see.

"Everything OK?" asked Franklin.

"Better than OK," Rose whispered. And she reached up to kiss him again, wrapping her arms around his neck.

"May I hug you before we part for the night?" asked Franklin respectfully.

"I would love that," said Rose in her dreamy state of mind.

"Good night, my beautiful Rose," Franklin said, taking her in his arms.

"Good night, Franklin, my Prince Charming," Rose replied as the two melted into each other.

They parted ways, both feeling sure that this felt like the real thing.

Rose started walking back to her apartment. There were only two more blocks to go as she thought nonstop about Franklin and the fun she had that night.

A black police officer in a campus patrol car stopped to ask if she was OK walking alone at night.

"Thanks," Rose said, "I'm fine. Only another block to go."

The officer waved and closed his window. He drove away slowly, but Rose felt his eyes on her from his rearview mirror.

"That was strange," Rose said to herself quietly. "But I guess that's his job. She shook her shoulders like she was shaking off spiderwebs as the memories of the past hit her.

Rose changed clothes, washed her face, and started to go to bed. It was 11:40 p.m., and she was tired but happy. Looking out of the front window, which faced the parking lot of her building, she noticed the same patrol car parked there. Feeling a strange jolt, she quickly closed the curtains and double-checked the door and all the windows to be sure they were locked before going to bed.

It seemed odd to her that the same officer who asked her if she was all right that night was parked in the lot of her apartment building. She wondered if something had happened on campus.

As she drifted off to sleep, Franklin was the only thing on her mind. "Good night, Prince Charming," she whispered, wrapping her arms around her shoulders in a tight hug.

SATURDAY MORNING, NOVEMBER 18ᵗʰ 1972

Rose's alarm went off at 9 a.m. Saturday morning. She saw sparkles of bright golden sunlight twinkling through the blinds on her bedroom window. That sight made it easy for her to jump out of bed and open the blinds. Franklin jumped into her thoughts immediately. She felt a heart full of love and hope and couldn't wait to tell Elenore.

She wondered why Elenore didn't wake her when she got home last night. Rose put on her slippers, quietly opened her door, and softly walked down the hall to Elenore's room. She saw the door was open and her bed was made.

"I wonder if she stayed with Tommy last night. I don't even have his phone number or address to check."

Rose started packing for her holiday visit to Chicago. By noon that day, she had not heard from Elenore.

Rose didn't want to leave until she knew Elenore was home and safe. Since she didn't feel comfortable leaving without knowing where Elenore was, she called the bus station to trade her bus ticket for Chicago from Saturday to Sunday.

Rose decided to call Franklin. "Good afternoon, Prince Charming," Rose said dreamily.

"Hello, beautiful," said Franklin.

Rose continued, "I'm worried, Elenore didn't come home last night. Do you have any idea where she would be? I was thinking that since she left with Tommy last night, maybe she stayed with him. But she has to leave for her holiday break later today. I think we might want to go look for her."

Franklin replied, "I don't know if she went home with Tommy, but I agree we should check some places. I'll drive over so we can make better time."

"OK, see you in a bit. Thank you," said Rose.

Franklin drove his 1965 maroon Chevy Impala to Rose's apartment building, parked, and went to her apartment.

He knocked on her door. Rose opened the door and hugged Franklin.

"Thank you so much for coming over. I never worry about Elenore because she is always so independent and smart, but she has never not come home at night," Rose told Franklin.

"Do you know what type of car Tommy drives?" asked Rose.

"I've seen him around campus in a green Barracuda that looks a few years old, maybe 1970," Franklin said. "Let's drive around the parks and places a couple might go."

"How well do you know TD?" asked Rose.

"Not very well, but I have heard he is a ladies' man. The girls really seem to go for him," Franklin said lightheartedly.

Rose chuckled, "I'm ready. I'll grab a flashlight, and then we can drive around looking for his car."

"Great, I have a flashlight in my glove compartment too,"

Franklin said.

Rose put on a light jacket over her sweater and jeans, grabbed a flashlight, and the two left in Franklin's car to find Elenore and TD.

TOMMY AND ELENORE NOV. 18th
1 a.m.

"Where are we going, Tommy?" asked Elenore.

"I know this little cozy place just a little way out of town. We can get one last beer and some breakfast," TD said. "How does that sound?"

Elenore replied, "That sounds just lovely. It's getting late, and I promised Rose I would be home around midnight."

"We'll head back right after, OK?" asked TD.

Elenore agreed with slight apprehension. "How much farther?" she asked.

"Just up ahead around the next curve," TD said, sounding odd.

They had been driving for fifteen minutes, and Elenore began to feel anxious. She saw no lights from a building or other cars headed this way. But she knew TD was a nice guy. She'd been out with him a few times, and he always treated her well.

"OK. I think it will be nice," said Elenore.

Five minutes later, Tommy rounded the curve. "Where is this place, Tommy?" implored Elenore.

"We have to get out and walk the pathway from here," said TD, sounding agitated.

"You mean through the woods?" asked Elenore. "I don't see a pathway. I have platform boots on. I don't think they'll make it through the woods."

"Then I guess I'll have to carry you," said TD with a sly smile.

Elenore tried to laugh and smile, but this was getting creepy. She wrapped her arms around herself and said, "TD, I'm getting a little spooked out here. Are you sure this is the right way?"

"It is. I've been here a few times before. The place is cool. It's like a little cabin out in the woods, then you go inside, and it's a great rocking bar and café," TD told her.

"If you say so," said Elenore, beginning to feel frightened.

"I'll park right here, and we can hike down this hill to the cabin," TD told Elenore.

Elenore's anxiety turned to full-on panic as she got full-body chills. Nothing about this felt right.

"Tommy, I don't want to hike down a hill in these shoes."

TD swept her up into his arms and started down the hill. Elenore could tell he'd been here before more than once. She kept her mind on his words, 'This place is cool. It's a rocking little bar and café.'

As they descended the wooded hill, TD put Elenore down on her feet and grabbed her hand. It felt like he was pulling her over the dirt and tree-root-covered ground as hard as possible. The first time she tripped and fell, he pulled her back up. She felt his hand yank her arm harder to keep her going.

She fell again and was covered with mud and leaves. "Tommy, where is this place? Where are you taking me?" Elenore cried.

At that remark, he pushed her down on the ground hard. "Look, El. Do you see a cabin around here?"

"No," she said, becoming more frightened and unnerved.

"No, there isn't a cabin here, but here we are anyway," TD said chillingly. "Let's make our own little party. And stop asking so many questions!"

Elenore put her hands down on the ground, trying to push herself away from him. He just stood over her like a skyscraper about to topple. She saw TD grab something from his jacket pocket. It gleamed in the moonlight, but she wasn't sure what it was or what was happening.

"Stop teasing me, El," said TD. "Why do they always tease me?"

Sitting on the forest floor, she pushed herself backward, away from him. Elenore said, "What do you mean, Tommy?"

He moved towards her like a rabid bear in the night.

ROSE AND FRANKLIN NOV. 18th
2:30 p.m.

"Look over there," said Franklin. "That looks like TD's car parked on the side of the road."

"Should we stop and look inside?" asked Rose.

"Yes, come on," Franklin said hurriedly.

The two parked in front of TD's car and peered through the windows.

"There's Elenore's purse on the seat," said Rose. "I told her not to forget it when they left the bar last night."

"Elenore, TD... Tommy," shouted Rose, her hands cupped around her mouth.

Franklin yelled forcefully, "Hey, TD, Elenore, are you here?"

With that loud noise from Franklin, they heard some rustling below just down the hill.

"Rose, can you hike with me down this hill?" asked Franklin.

"Yes, I want to find Elenore," said Rose emphatically.

Franklin and Rose started down the wooded hill. It was still light out, but it was darker down the hill. Franklin also brought a flashlight, which he kept in his glove compartment. They grabbed their flashlights and shone them down the hill in different directions.

"We have about two hours before it will start to get dark. We can cover a lot of ground in that amount of time," said Franklin.

"Hey, did you hear that?" asked Rose. I hear some rustling down there. Like someone or something is moving."

"Yes, I hear it." Franklin said, " Let's go that way."

"What if they are hurt or something?" Rose asked, concerned.

Slowly descending the hill together, they noticed broken branches and shoe prints in the dirt.

"Oh, Franklin, there is Elenore's jacket," said Rose, sounding uneasy.

"Remember not to touch anything. Let's keep looking," Franklin instructed.

The next thing they saw was spine-chilling and gruesome.

Elenore's lifeless body was on the ground, face up. Her clothes were utterly disheveled. Her skirt and Rose's peasant blouse were sliced to pieces. One of her boots was missing, and the other boot was lying two feet away from her body. Her jacket was flung to the place where Rose saw it.

She was covered in blood from what looked like stab wounds to her neck, chest, arms, and torso. Her neck had been slashed from one side to the other, almost decapitating her.

Rose screamed, "NO, what happened?" as she broke down, her entire body shuddering.

Franklin dropped to his knees. The flashlight fell from his hands as he covered his mouth.

"We have to go back to town and call the police," cried Rose, not knowing whether to scream or whisper.

"Where is TD?" asked Franklin. "We should go look for him."

Rose replied nervously, "Let's see if we can find him, then go to the police."

They got to their feet and walked farther down the hill, only to find TD slumped against a tree with a hunting knife at his side. He was covered in blood but was alive. It didn't look like he had been stabbed, but someone undeniably put up a fight with him. His face was scratched and scraped. It appeared that he had been punched and possibly hit with a rock to his right temple.

"Let's go now!" said Franklin frantically.

Rose and Franklin went to the car as fast as possible. They drove the backroads to the city and right to the police station.

When they entered the station, the officer at the front desk knew something was terribly wrong.

"What happened?" asked the officer.

"We went to look for my roommate, who never came home last night. She went on a date with a new boyfriend and never got home," Rose said, almost hoarse from fright.

Franklin added, "We decided to drive around and see if we could find them. I know his car, so we drove around looking for it. We saw it parked on the side of the road in a wooded area. We looked in the car windows and saw Rose's roommate's purse inside on the passenger seat. So we hiked down the hill in the woods. And what we found was...was..." Franklin swallowed and felt bile rising. He couldn't complete the sentence.

The officer said, "Take your time, sir."

Rose was gasping, "Elenore is dead, and TD is hurt badly."

Franklin was able to continue, "Can someone come to the scene? We can lead you to the area. And we need an ambulance."

JIMMY FEBRUARY 1973

With Burrows, Ray Davis, and Delores behind bars and fully recovered, Jimmy was ready to meet with Officer Robinson about his new community plan.

"Jimmy, thanks for meeting with me. What would you think about training to become a police officer?"

Jimmy looked up at Officer Robinson, "Really? Become an officer, for real?"

"Yes, for real," said Officer Robinson. "I am forming the African American Patrolman's League, or AAPL for short. The goal is to bring civil rights suits against the CPD for discrimination against minorities – Blacks and Latinos. I'm hoping to get Sebastian Ortiz on board as well. It's going to turn your life around and his, and help so many in our communities."

"I would be honored to join you, Officer Robinson. What is the next step?"

"After you fill out the application forms, we'll get you into police training in the next academy starting April 2nd. I will be your training officer. After you complete your rookie training, you will be in a class of Black and Latino officers training on police brutality and racial profiling against Black community members. The AAPL is fighting for better relations between the police and the Black and Brown community to improve safety and trust within neighborhoods," said Officer Robinson.

"We need this. After Burrows and the others, people need to feel safe," Jimmy said with heartfelt sincerity.

"I'm heading over to speak with Sebastian Oritz and his parents. Would you like to come?" asked Officer Robinson.

"Yes, sure, I would," said Jimmy, feeling like he had a future.

TOMMY AND ELENORE NOV. 18th 5:10 p.m. 1972

Rose and Franklin led officers to the scene, where they found Elenore and TD. The police arrived with search dogs, lights, and weapons. Everything they found was bagged as evidence. They saw Elenore just as Rose and Franklin described. But there was something that wasn't at the scene: Tommy D. Stone.

"Officers, TD was leaning up against this tree. He's gone. I thought he was dead or close to it," Franklin said urgently. "And the hunting knife we saw is gone too."

"Radio for an ambulance for Elenore," said the officer in charge of the search. Tell them she is deceased and will need the medical examiner."

"Frank, where did TD go? How did he get away?" asked Rose, trying to piece this together.

"I don't know. He was in pretty bad shape. I wasn't sure he was even alive," Franklin said. "Maybe someone dragged him off. Could that even happen?"

The officer in charge told Rose and Franklin to go home and that they would be in touch as soon as possible.

Rose said to Franklin, "I don't want to leave. They have to find him."

Franklin wrapped his arm around Rose's shoulder and said, "Let's go home. The police will be sure to tell us anything we should know."

Rose and Franklin walked back up the hill to the car. "Oh, Franklin, I have to let Elenore's mother know," said Rose as she stopped walking and turned to Franklin, taking his arm.

Franklin replied, "I know. But let's wait until they tell us it's OK to do that."

Rose nodded and began to cry. Suddenly, they both heard a strange noise from the opposite direction of the police movement and lights. Franklin turned quickly to look.

"What was that?" Rose asked, distressed.

"It sounded like someone running, or some animal," said Franklin as he spotted a figure in the dark in the beam of his flashlight.

"Rose, let's get back to the car," said Franklin cautiously.

They hiked up the hill to Franklin's car, but TD's car was no longer parked where it had been.

"Where is TD's car? Was he in any shape to drive?" asked Franklin.

"What is going on?" asked Rose as cold, hard shivers rushed through her like an earthquake.

ROSE AND FRANKLIN NOV. 18th
7:30 p.m. 1972

"Hello, Mama?"

"Yes, Rose. Are you all right? We've been worried about you since you were supposed to be on your way home," said Mrs. Williams.

Rose hesitated to breathe, then composed herself to speak, "Mama, something awful has happened. It's Elenore."

Mrs. Williams spoke, "What happened, Rose? Is Elenore all right?"

Rose could barely get the words out, "No, Mama, she is not all right." Rose's voice became cracked and shaky. " It's a long story, but she was murdered last night. Oh, Mama, it's so shocking. We found her."

"Oh no, Rose! Can you tell me what happened, sweetheart?" asked Mrs. Williams. "And are you safe?"

"Yes, Mama, I'm safe, and Franklin is here. Elenore didn't come home from her date last night, so I called Franklin to come over so we could go look for her," Rose said, staying calm.

"Go on, baby," said Mrs. Williams.

"She went on a date with a new boyfriend named Tommy. I don't know him, but she's been out with him a few other times. She didn't come home this morning, and it looked like she hadn't been here at all since we left to go out last night. I thought maybe she stayed with him last night."

Rose continued losing her calm voice, "This morning we went to look for her and drove around everywhere we could think of. We decided to drive to the wooded area off campus to look for Tommy's car. We found his car parked at the top of a wooded hill. We saw Elenore's purse on the seat of his car."

Rose stopped to breathe and gather her thoughts. The next part was the most difficult to tell.

"Franklin and I hiked down the hill and...Mama, I don't know how to tell you this," Rose gasped and took a deep breath.

"Go on, honey, go on," said Mrs. Williams

Catching her breath and holding back her tears, Rose said, "We found her jacket lying on the ground. Then, farther down the hill, we saw Elenore. Someone had brutally attacked her. She had been stabbed and assaulted. We looked for Tommy. He was leaning up against a tree with a hunting knife beside him. We thought he was dead, too."

Then, letting out a breath she didn't even know she had been holding, Rose continued, "We hurried back to the car to go to the police. After we told them what we found, we led them to the scene. When we got there, Tommy's car was gone, and so was he. Mama, I am so afraid."

Mrs. Williams said, "Rose, do the police need you to stay and give statements?"

"Yes, Mama," said Rose. "So I changed my ticket to leave tomorrow, but I think I'll have to move it one more day. We're waiting for the police to call so we can give our statements, then I can come home."

"Mama, can you call Iris and Lily to let them know?"

"Yes, Rose. I will certainly do that. Please keep in touch so I know you're safe and on the way home! I love you, my Rose."

"I love you too, Mama."

Rose and Franklin waited to hear from the police. At 10 p.m., the phone rang, making Rose and Franklin jump.

"Hello," said Rose.

"Is this Rose Williams?" said a voice on the other end.

"Yes, this is Rose."

"Miss Williams, this is Officer Tate at the DC Police Department. Are you and Franklin Harris available to come to the station near campus to give a statement tonight?"

"Yes, we've been waiting for your call. We'll be there in a few minutes," confirmed Rose.

Rose hung up the phone, and it rang again immediately. She answered. A male voice on the other end asked, "Is Elenore there?"

Rose handed the phone to Franklin with a panicked look in her eyes.

"Who is this?" he asked.

The caller hung up.

Rose and Franklin headed to the police station and didn't wait to figure out who was calling. Rose made sure her window blinds were closed. She glanced out to see the usual cars parked in her apartment lot. That police car was there too.

"Franklin, before we go to the station, I want to ask the officer why he has been parked in my lot lately," Rose told Franklin.

"Let's do that. It feels like he's guarding something," Franklin said.

Rose approached the patrol car, signaling the officer to roll down his window.

"Hello, Miss, can I help you?" he asked.

"Why have you been here so often, and why did you ask if I needed help when I was walking home last night?" Rose inquired.

The officer responded, "We've been getting a lot of reports of unfortunate events in the campus area. I'm here for your safety."

"Thank you," Rose replied. "It's appreciated."

"It's my job, ma'am. I'm glad you're safe. If you see or hear anything odd, please call the station," the officer told Rose and Franklin.

Rose and Franklin looked at each other and got in Franklin's car.

"This has been a very long night," said Rose, exhausted.

"And I don't think it's over yet," replied Franklin.

www.ingramcontent.com/pod-product-compliance
Lightning Source LLC
Chambersburg PA
CBHW041050310726
48978CB00011BA/492